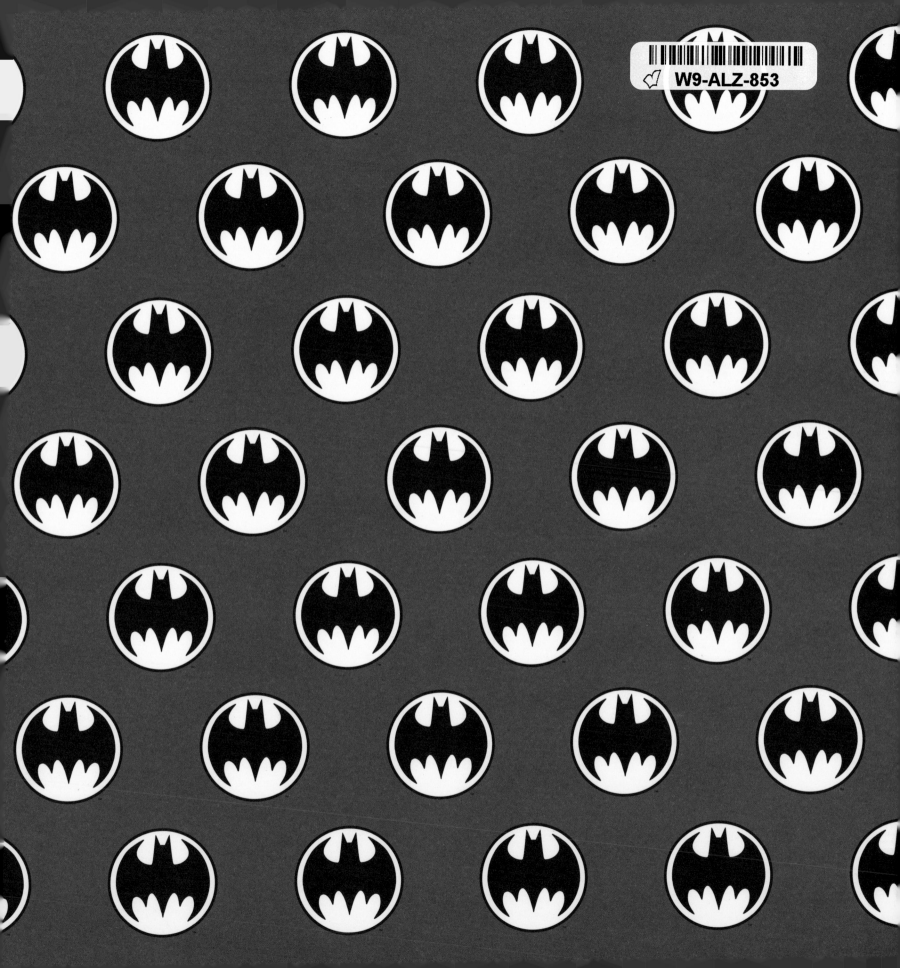

THE BIG BOOK OF
BATMAN™

by Noah Smith

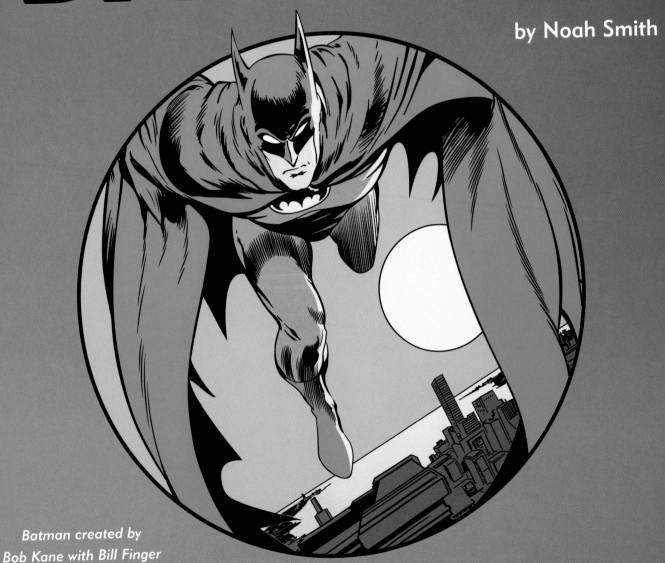

Batman created by
Bob Kane with Bill Finger

downtown bookworks

downtown bookworks

Downtown Bookworks Inc.
265 Canal Street
New York, New York 10013
www.downtownbookworks.com

Designed by Georgia Rucker
Typeset in Geometric and CCHeroSandwich

Printed in China
July 2017
ISBN 978-1-941367-46-9
10 9 8 7 6 5 4 3 2 1

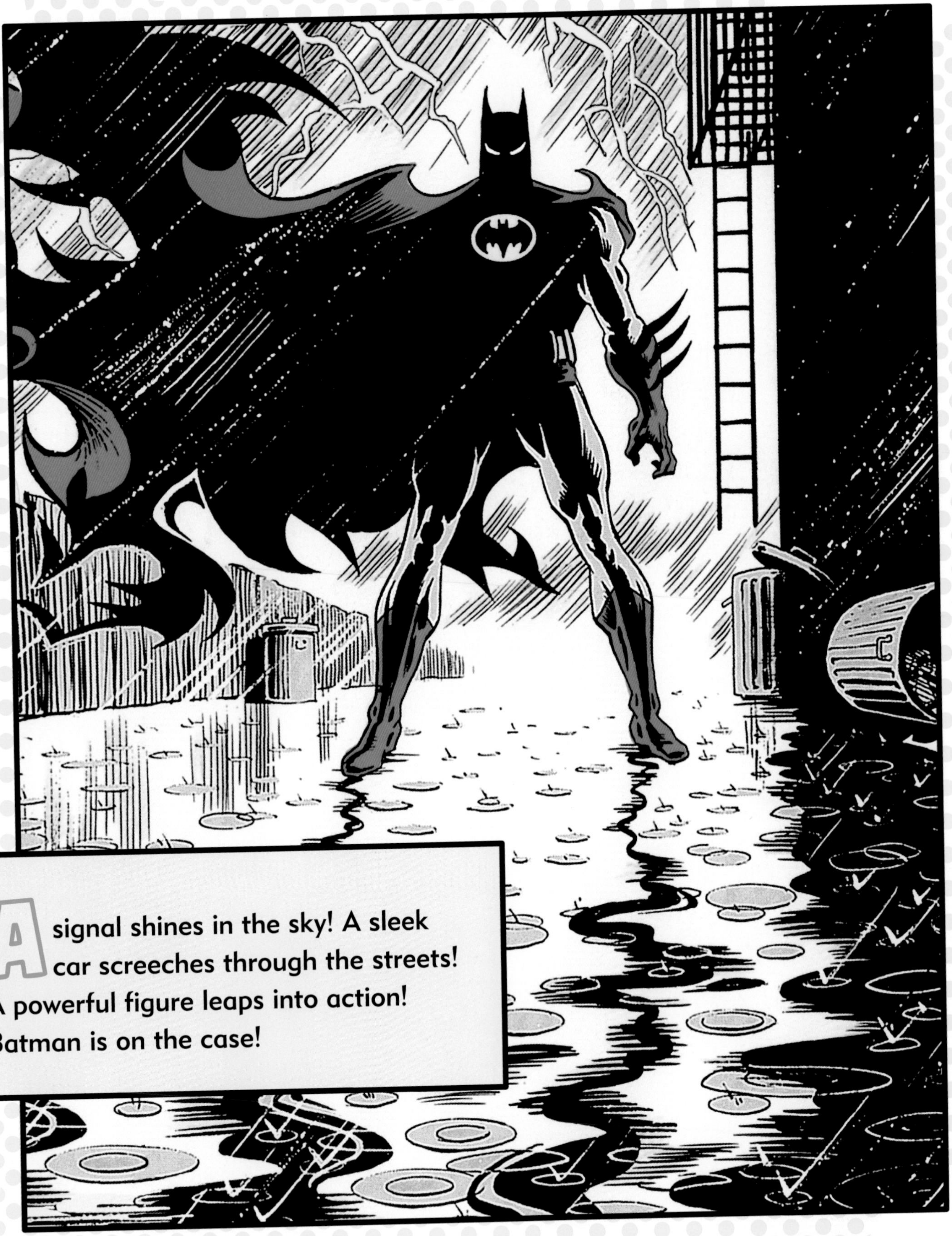

A signal shines in the sky! A sleek car screeches through the streets! A powerful figure leaps into action! Batman is on the case!

A DARK NIGHT

Batman's story has a sad beginning. Bruce Wayne was the young son of the richest family in Gotham City. But when he lost his parents during a robbery, his perfect world crumbled.

Sad, scared, and angry, Bruce swore that he would devote his life to fighting crime.

Young Bruce exercised to strengthen his body. And he read as much as he could to strengthen his mind. In college, he studied chemistry, physics, engineering, history, psychology, and other subjects. Then, he traveled the world to learn even more.

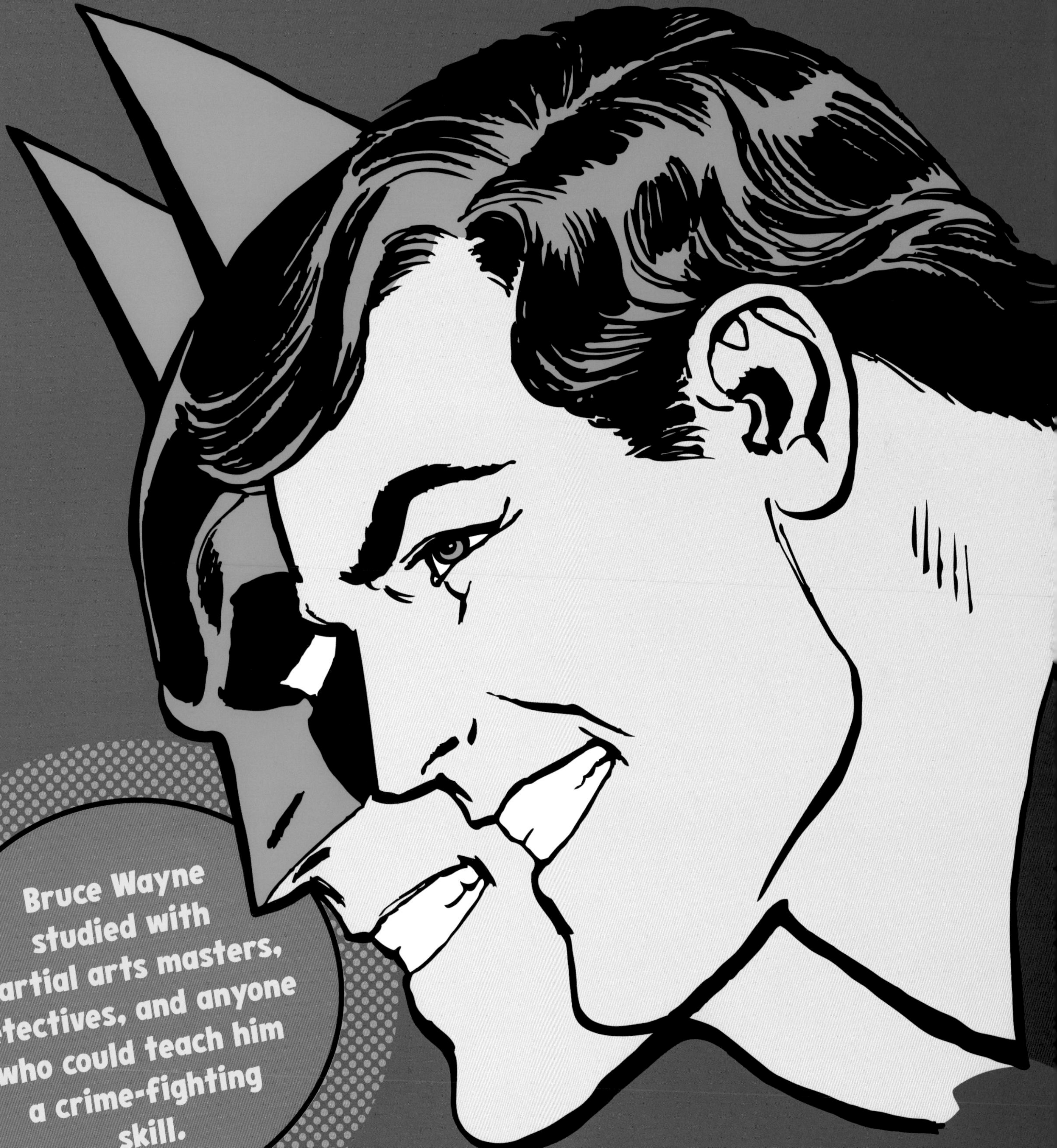

Bruce Wayne studied with martial arts masters, detectives, and anyone who could teach him a crime-fighting skill.

THE DARK KNIGHT

When he returned to Gotham City, Bruce felt like he was ready. But he needed something more. He needed a special identity.

Could he create a disguise? A look that would scare the cowardly criminals the way they tried to scare their victims? Late one evening, a bat flew in through an open window. Bruce was inspired. "I must be a creature of the night," he said to himself.

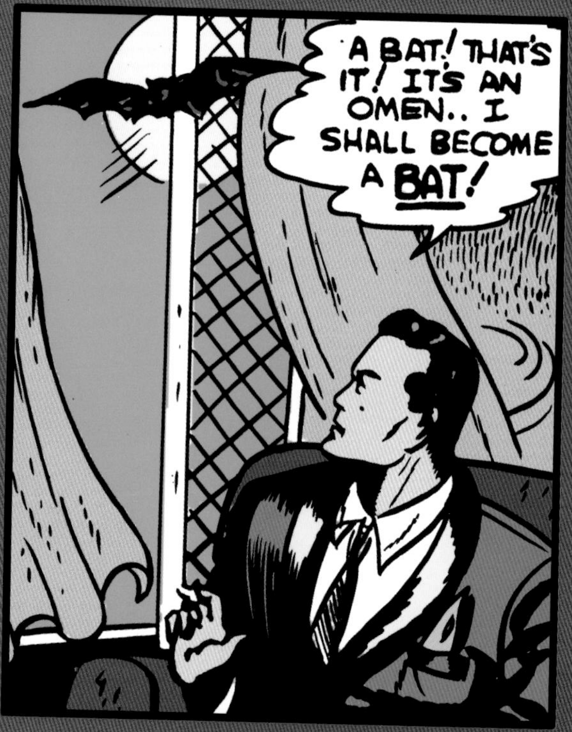
A BAT! THAT'S IT! ITS AN OMEN.. I SHALL BECOME A BAT!

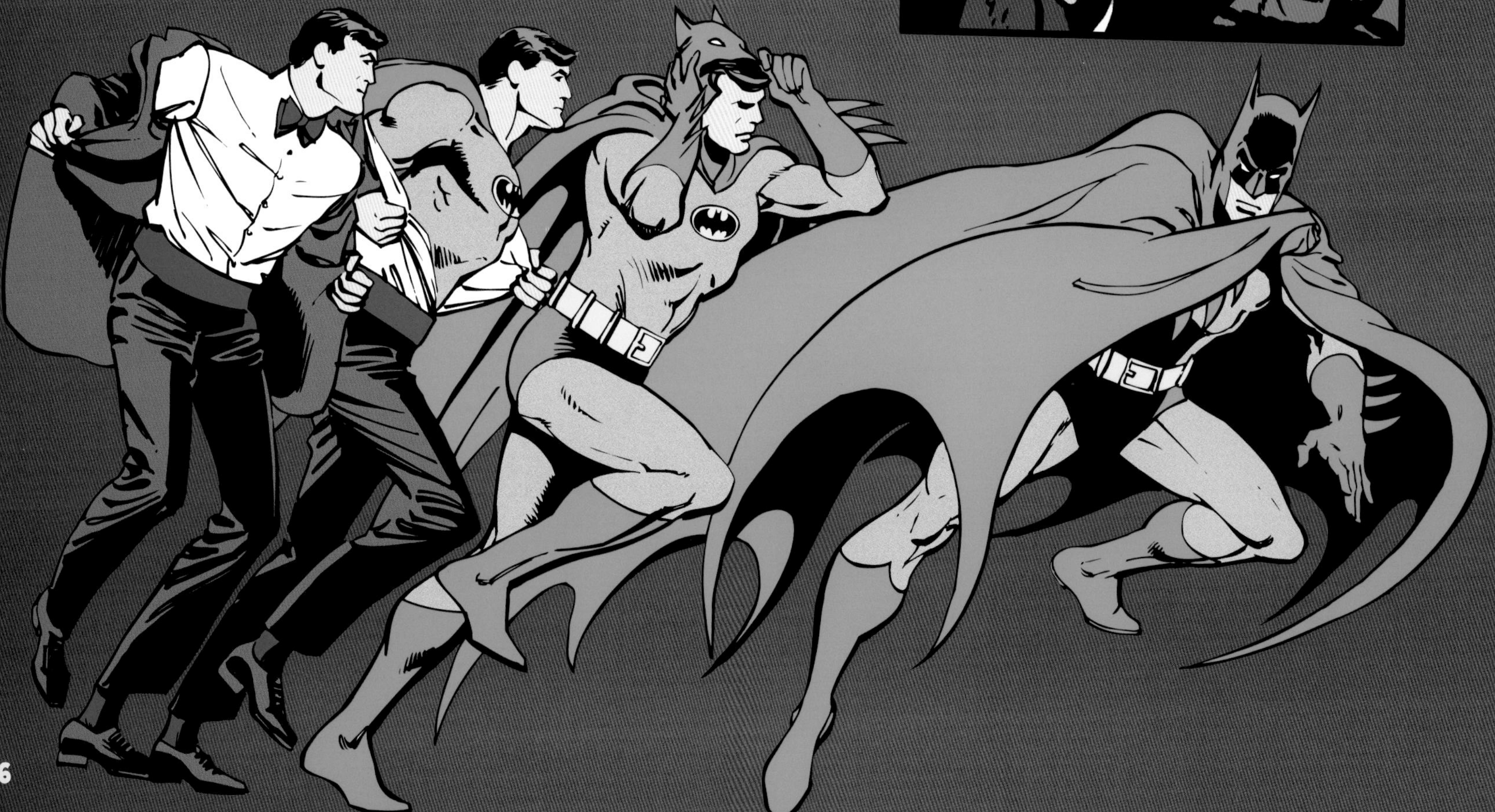

Bruce designed a costume that would strike terror into the hearts of anyone trying to do harm. Gotham City had a new protector—Batman!

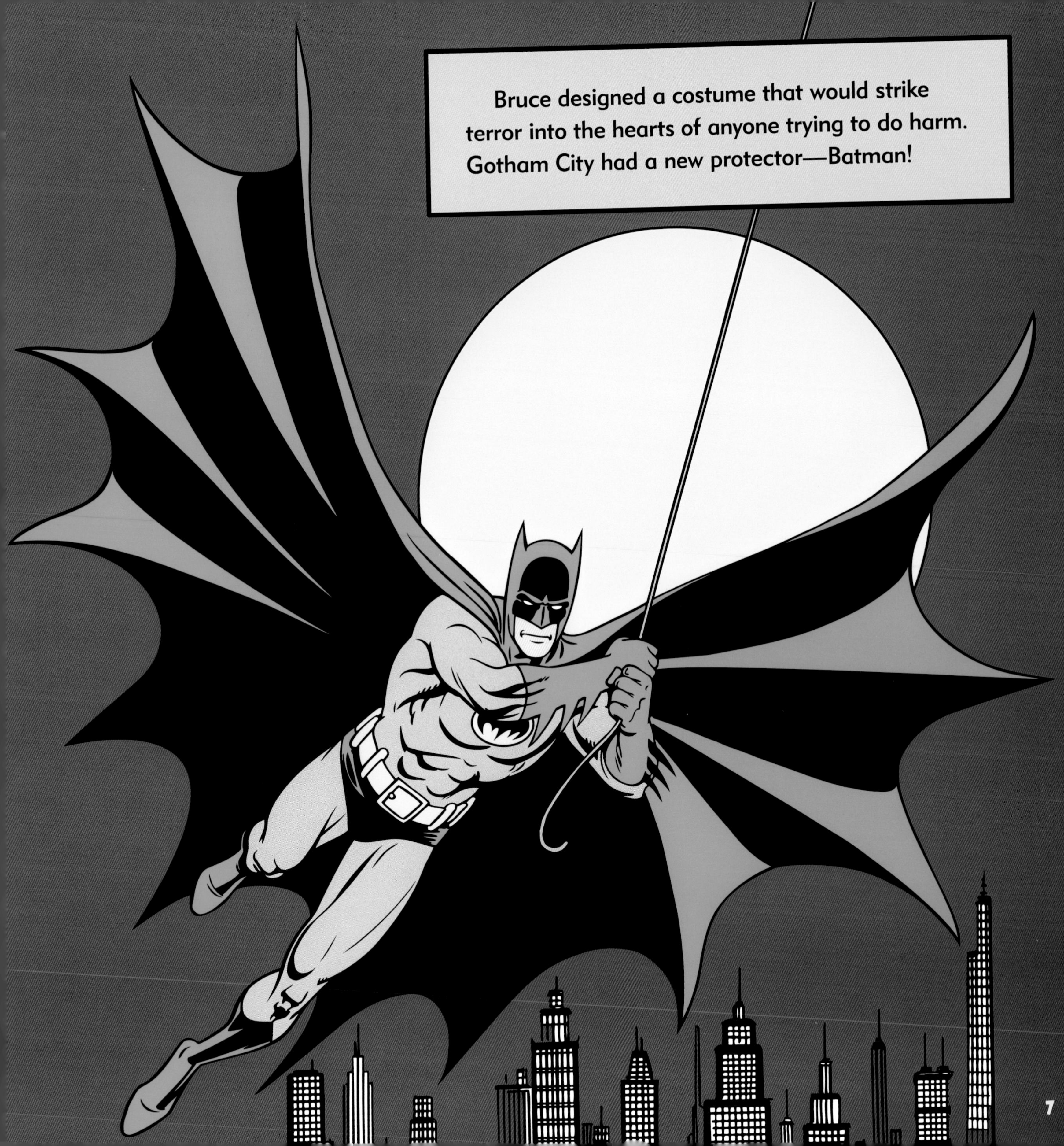

HOW DOES A MAN BECOME A BATMAN?

Unlike many super heroes, Batman has no superpowers. But he is as strong, fast, and agile as any champion athlete. And he mastered more than 100 forms of martial arts to create his own unique fighting style.

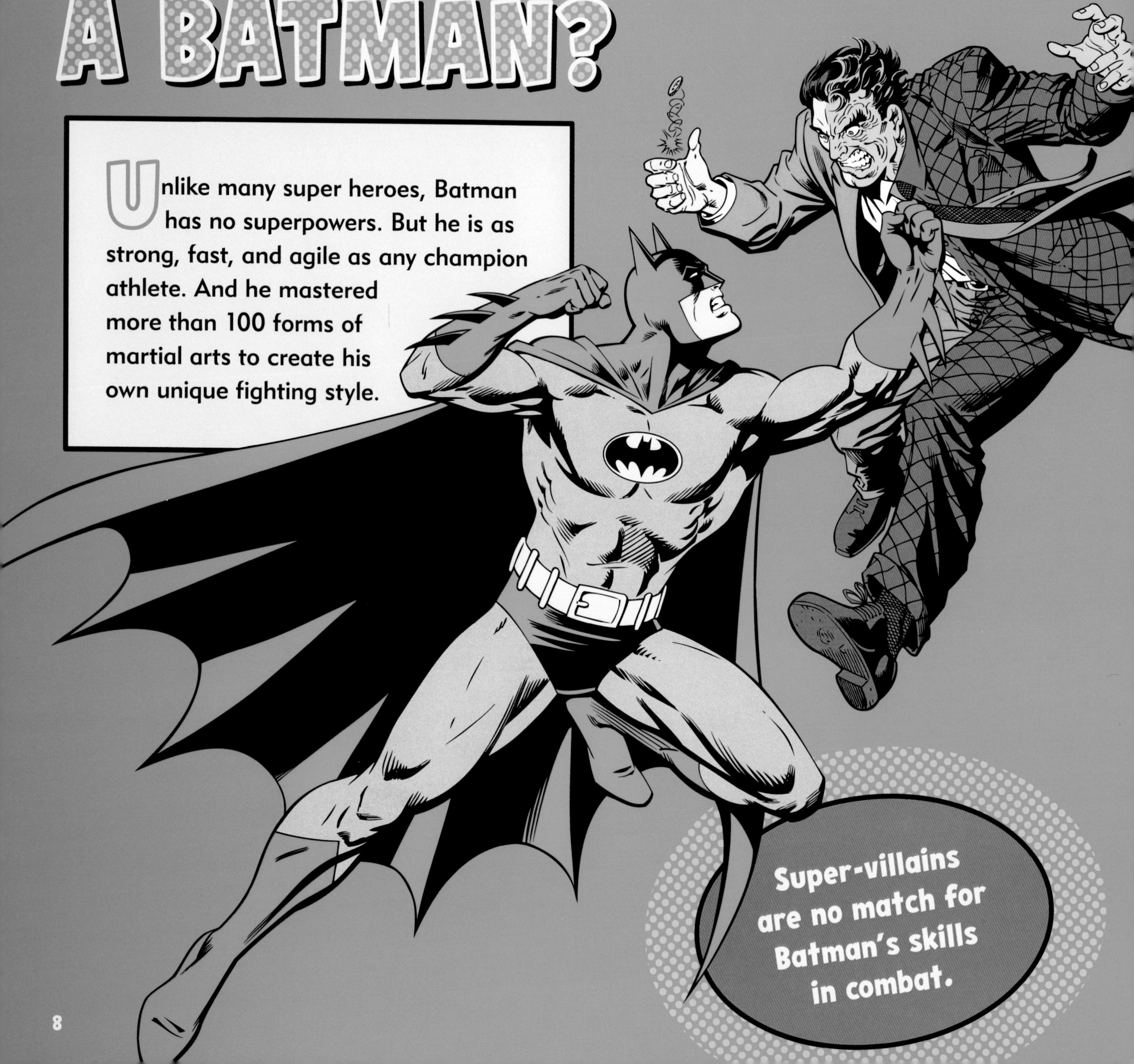

Super-villains are no match for Batman's skills in combat.

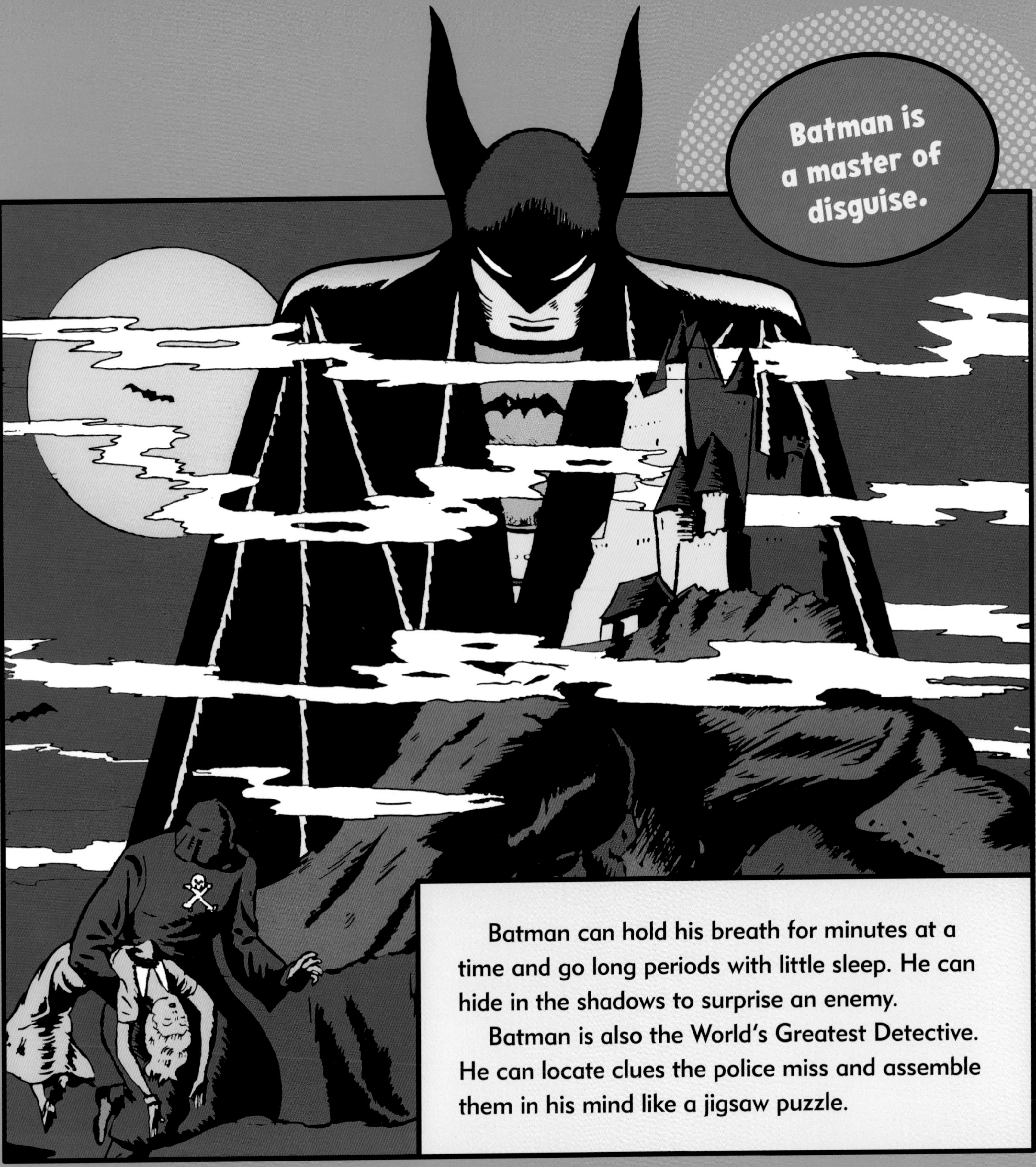

Batman is a master of disguise.

Batman can hold his breath for minutes at a time and go long periods with little sleep. He can hide in the shadows to surprise an enemy.

Batman is also the World's Greatest Detective. He can locate clues the police miss and assemble them in his mind like a jigsaw puzzle.

HIDDEN HEADQUARTERS

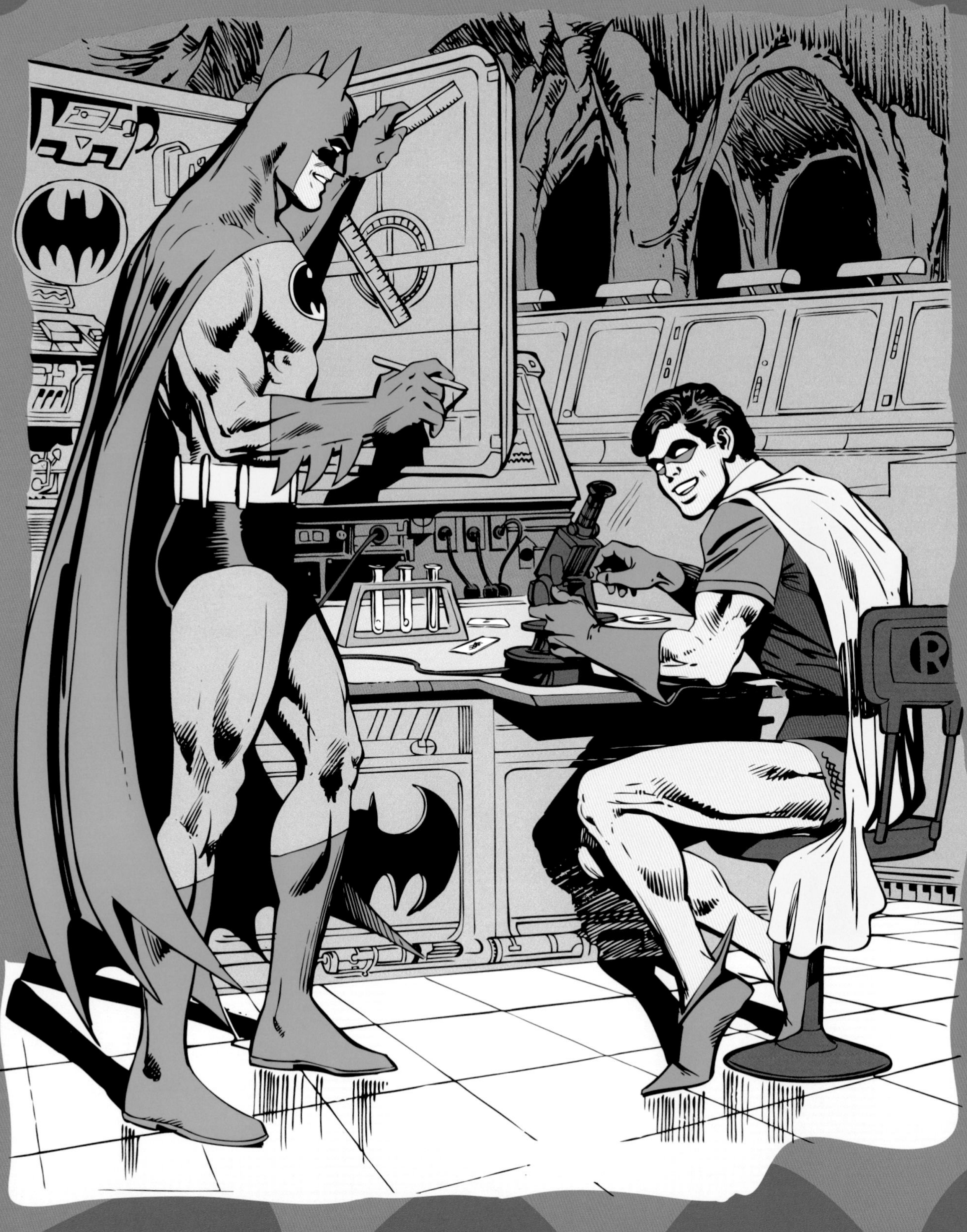

Bruce lives in Wayne Manor, a stately mansion. Beneath his elegant home is an enormous natural cavern. Batman transformed this cave into his base of operations.

The Batcave is full of spare costumes, weapons, exercise equipment, and trophies from his craziest cases. It is also home to the Batcomputer, an incredible machine that Batman uses to help unravel the toughest mysteries.

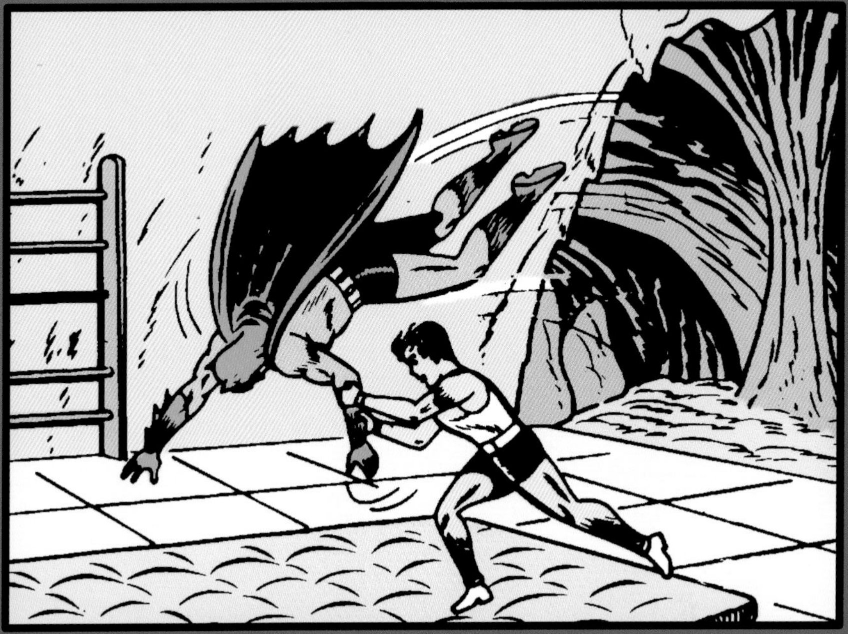

To keep his underground hideout secure, Batman enters the Batcave through a secret passage or hidden tunnels that only the Batmobile can navigate.

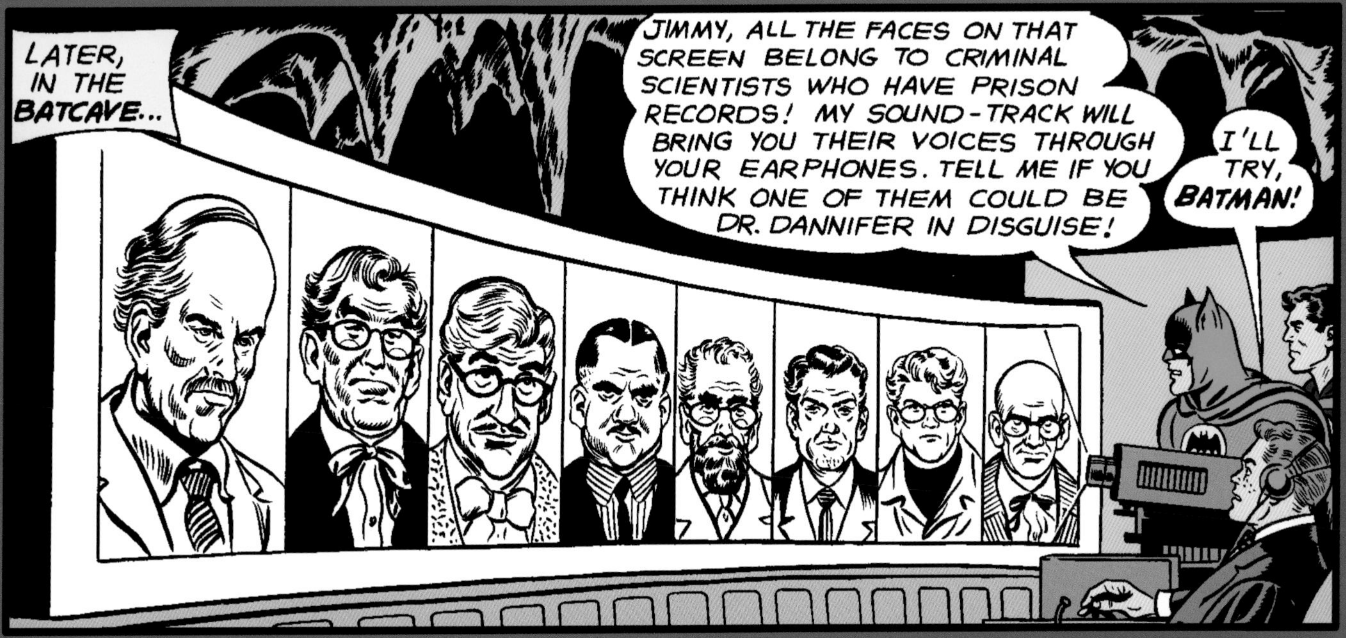
LATER, IN THE BATCAVE...
JIMMY, ALL THE FACES ON THAT SCREEN BELONG TO CRIMINAL SCIENTISTS WHO HAVE PRISON RECORDS! MY SOUND-TRACK WILL BRING YOU THEIR VOICES THROUGH YOUR EARPHONES. TELL ME IF YOU THINK ONE OF THEM COULD BE DR. DANNIFER IN DISGUISE!
I'LL TRY, BATMAN!

BUCKLE UP!

More than just the coolest vehicle in the world, the Batmobile is the ultimate crook-catching car. It is faster than any race car, and it is loaded with gadgets. It even has a lab inside!

The Batmobile is always ready to roar into action!

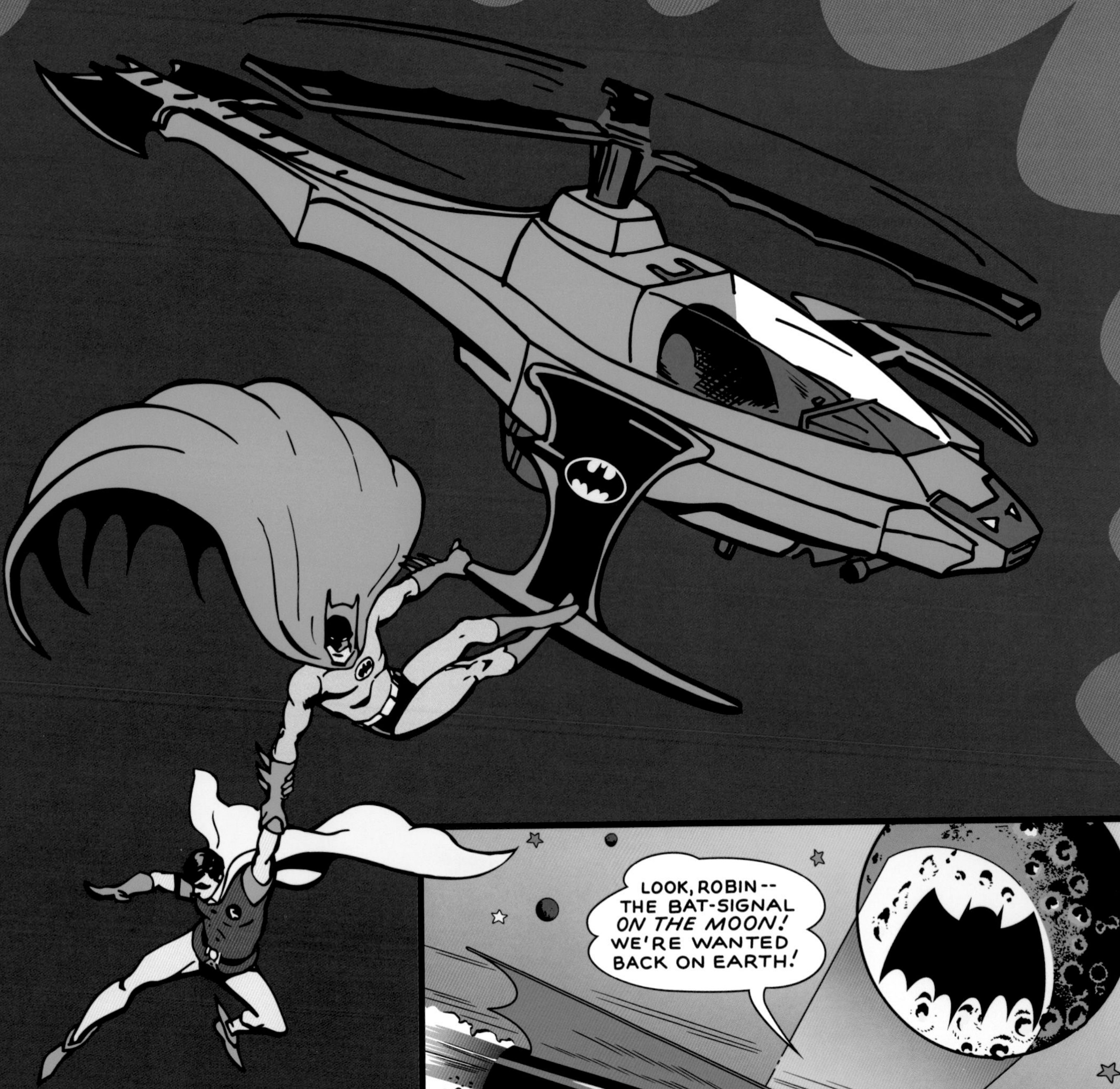

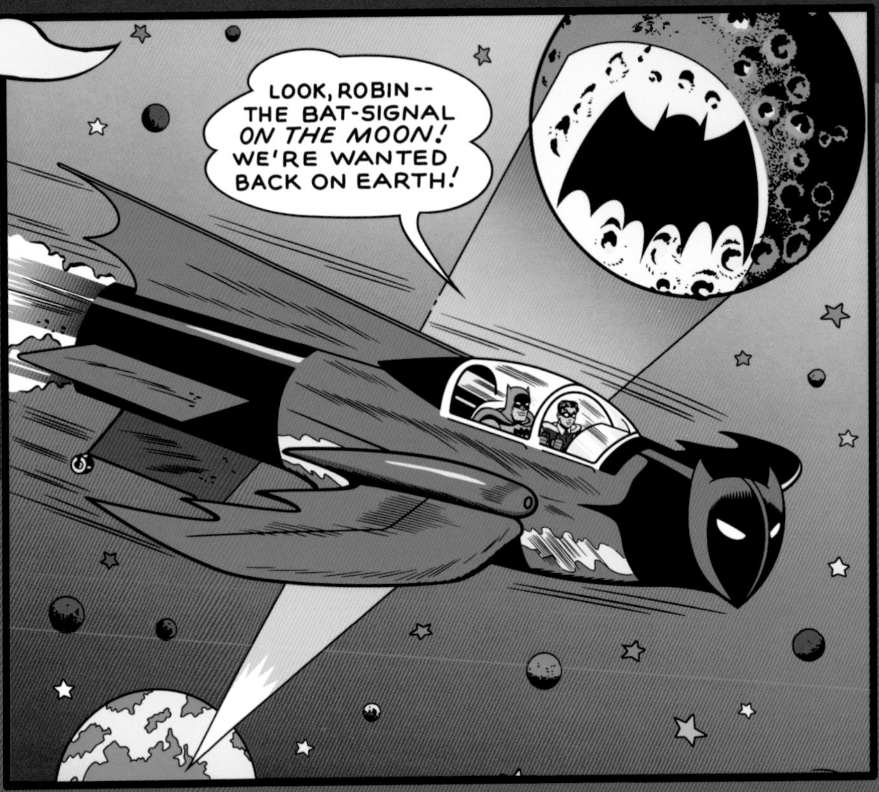
LOOK, ROBIN-- THE BAT-SIGNAL *ON THE MOON!* WE'RE WANTED BACK ON EARTH!

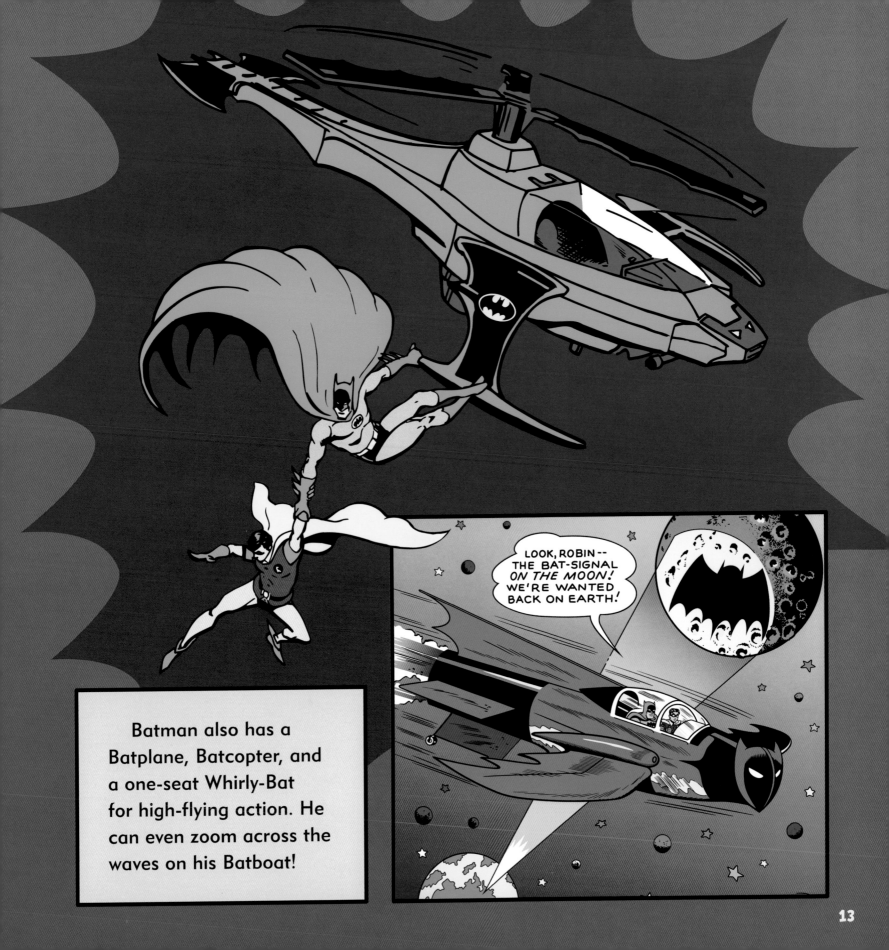

Batman also has a Batplane, Batcopter, and a one-seat Whirly-Bat for high-flying action. He can even zoom across the waves on his Batboat!

SAVED BY THE BELT

Batman wears a Utility Belt full of the tools and gear he needs to fight crime. He never leaves the Batcave without it! Batman stocks his belt with smoke bombs, pellets of knockout gas, and more.

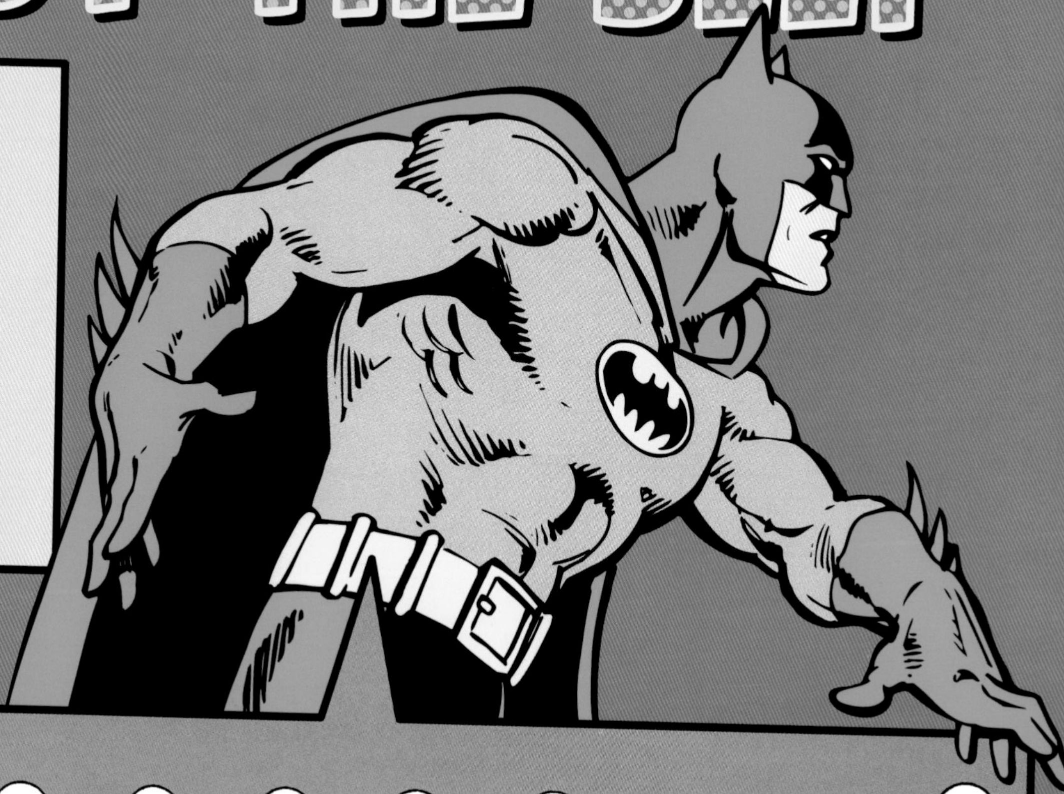

UTILITY BELT

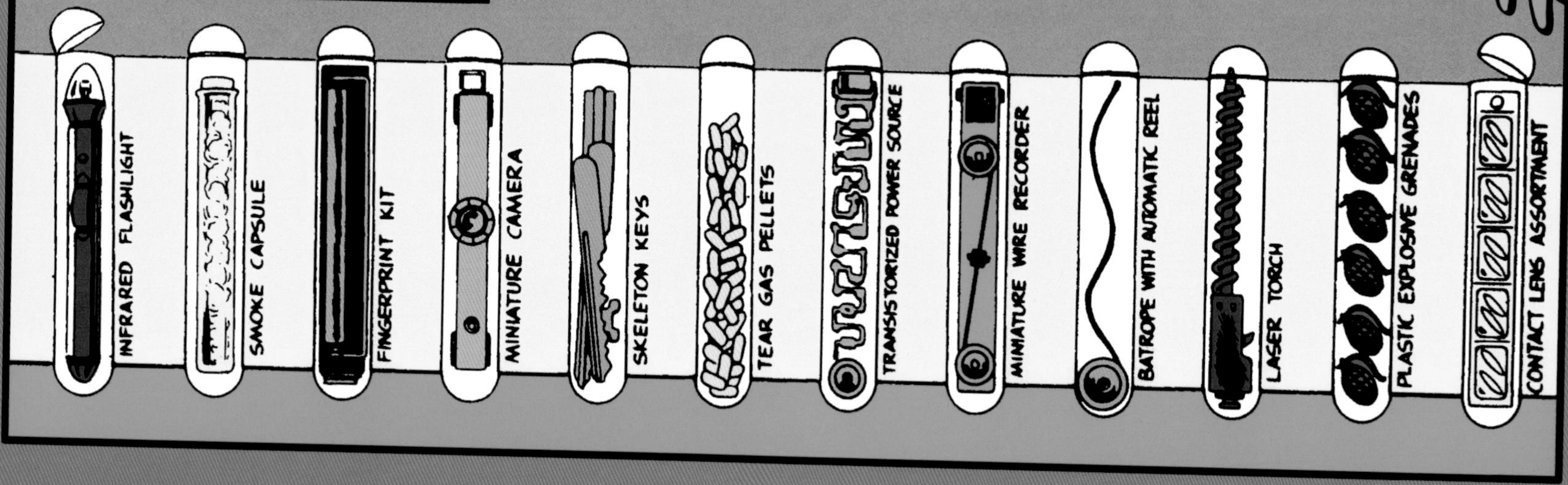

INFRARED FLASHLIGHT
SMOKE CAPSULE
FINGERPRINT KIT
MINIATURE CAMERA
SKELETON KEYS
TEAR GAS PELLETS
TRANSISTORIZED POWER SOURCE
MINIATURE WIRE RECORDER
BATROPE WITH AUTOMATIC REEL
LASER TORCH
PLASTIC EXPLOSIVE GRENADES
CONTACT LENS ASSORTMENT

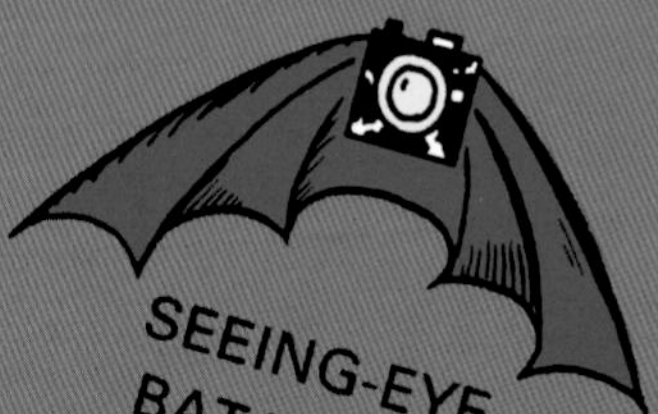

SEEING-EYE BATARANG

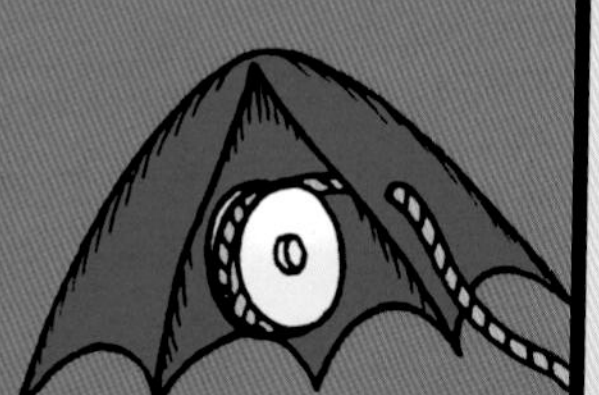

ROPE BATARANG

The Batarang is a special kind of boomerang. Batman can hurl it around corners or across great distances. Some special Batarangs carry electric shocks, magnets, or other gadgets.

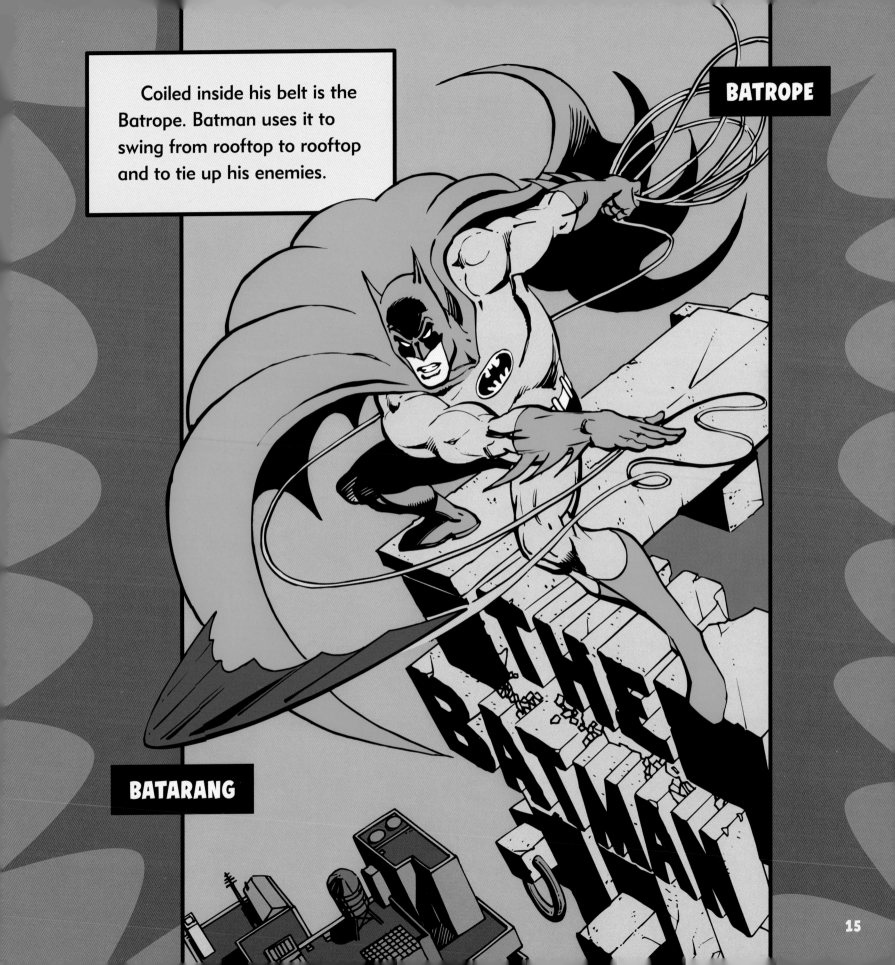

Coiled inside his belt is the Batrope. Batman uses it to swing from rooftop to rooftop and to tie up his enemies.

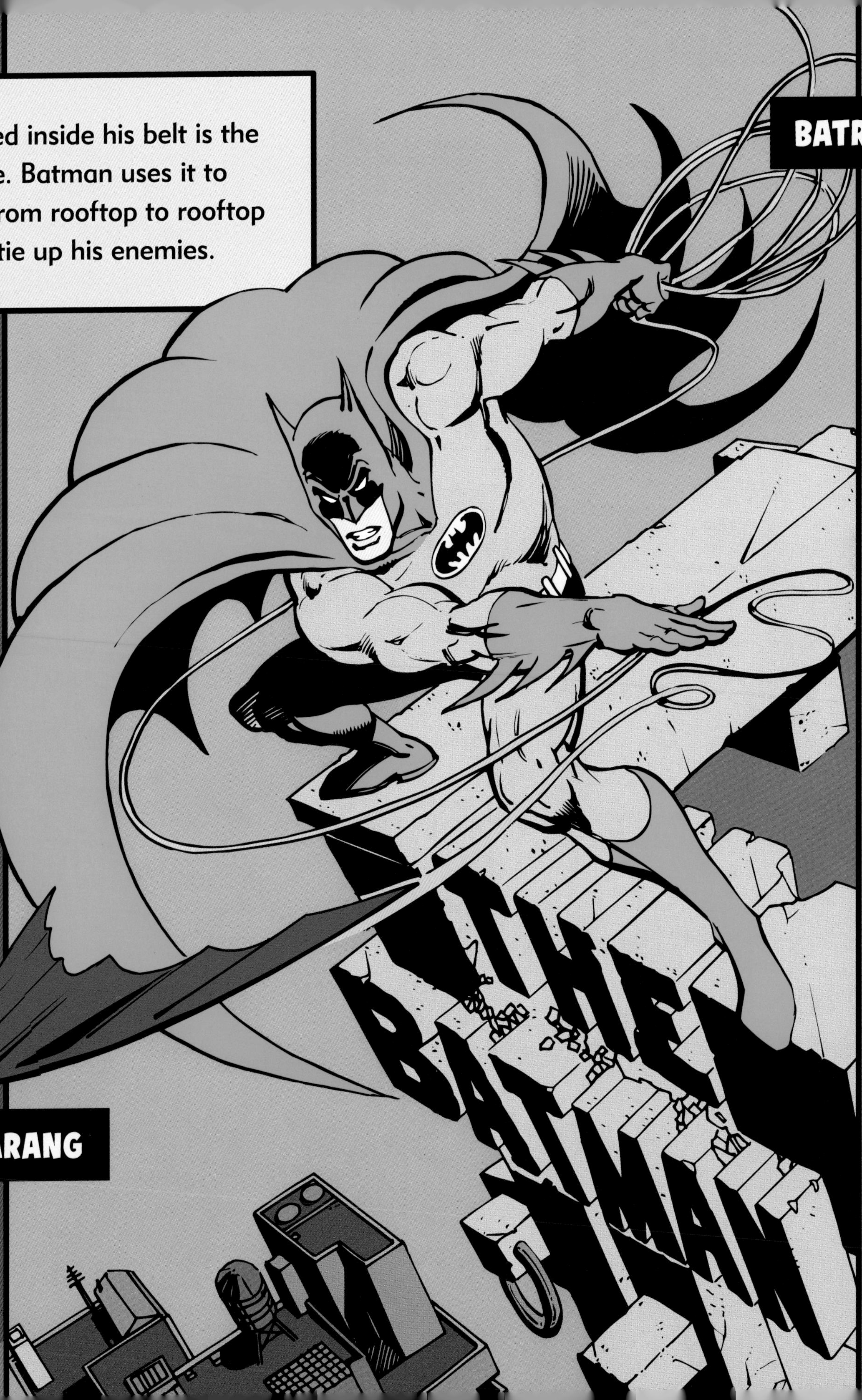
BATROPE
BATARANG
THE BATMAN

BILLIONAIRE BRUCE

When he's not in costume, Bruce Wayne runs an enormous company called Wayne Industries. To disguise his identity, Bruce lets the world think he's just a handsome billionaire. He pretends he is only interested in parties and vacations. But behind the scenes, Bruce is a clever businessman. He makes sure his company earns money fairly and responsibly.

THAT CHANDELIER SUDDENLY GLOWING... IT'S THE **BATCAVE** ALARM... SOMEONE'S DOWN THERE!

ONLY **SUPERMAN** KNOWS ITS SECRET... IF IT'S NOT **SUPERMAN**, IT'S TROUBLE! GET INTO COSTUME FAST, DICK!

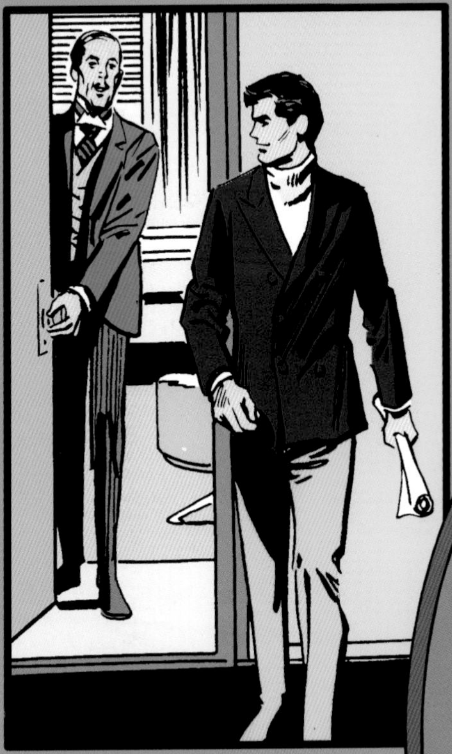

Alfred Pennyworth is Bruce's butler. Alfred keeps Wayne Manor running smoothly. He is also Bruce's oldest friend and greatest adviser. His wisdom and experience have helped crack many a case. Batman trusts Alfred with all his secrets.

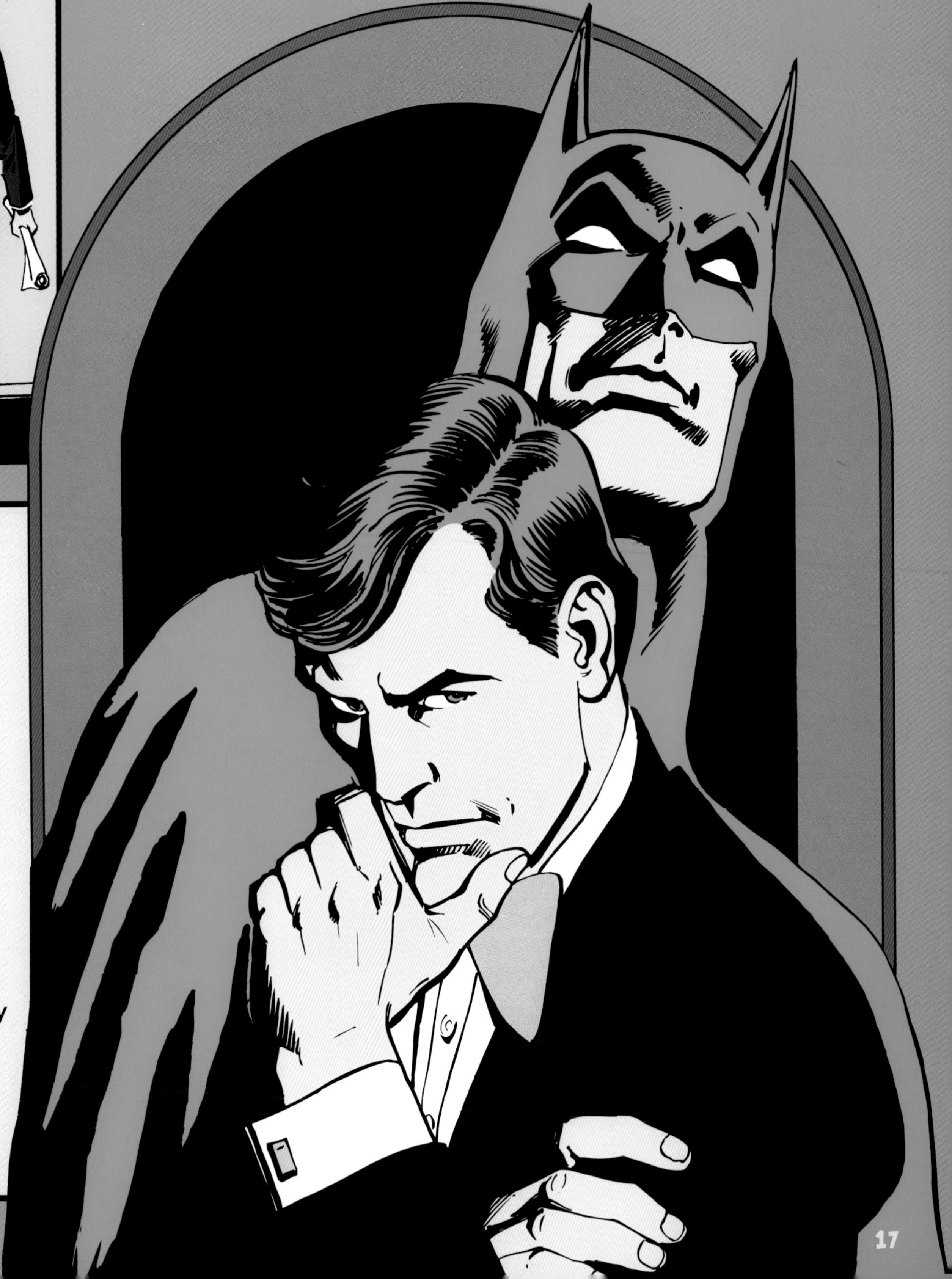

THE BOY WONDER

Like Batman, Dick Grayson lost his parents to crime. He was a young circus acrobat, and he felt the same thirst for justice that Batman did. Bruce Wayne adopted him and trained him to be a hero. The two spent many long hours exercising and studying together. And then Batman had a new partner—Robin!

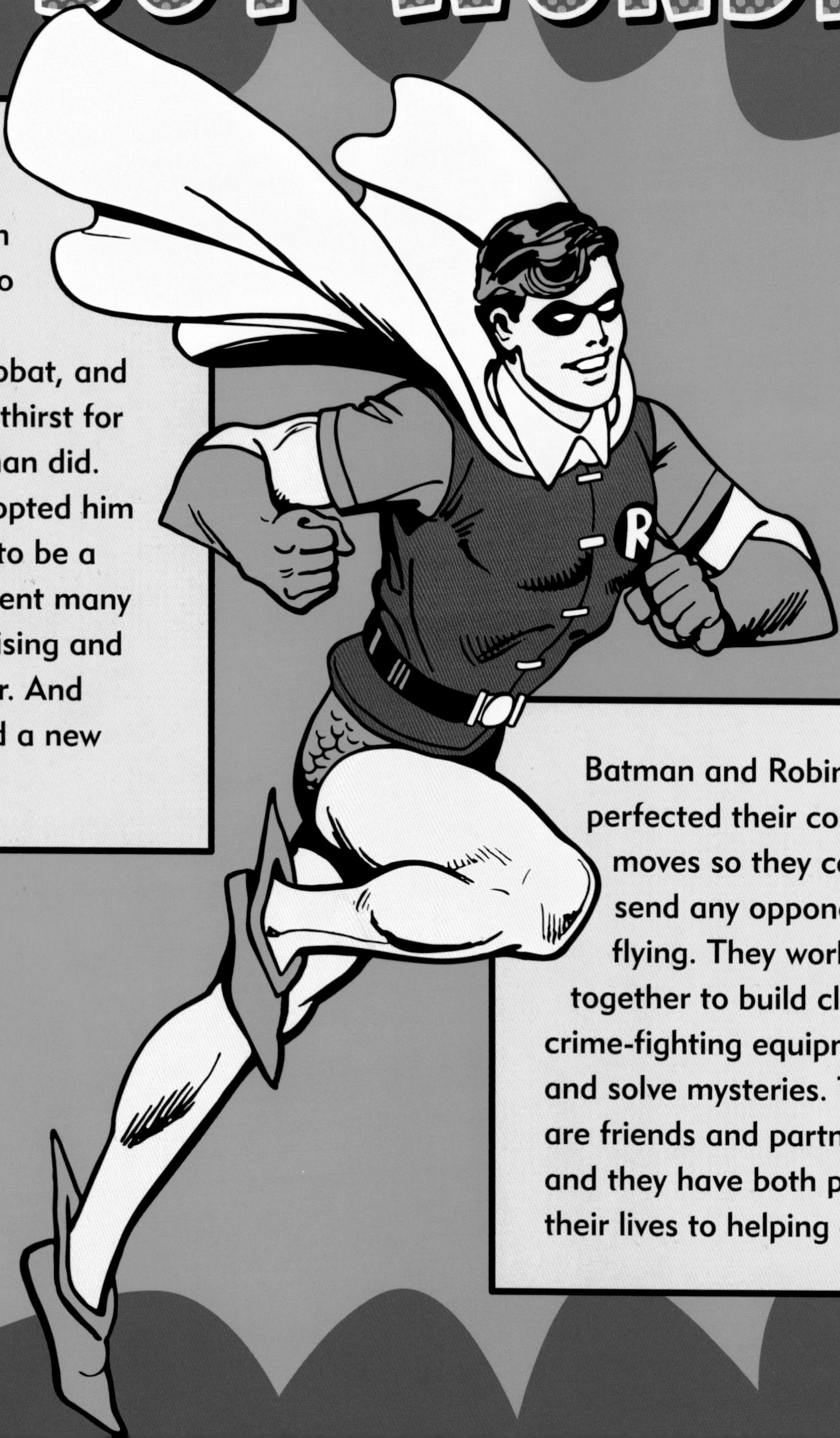

Batman and Robin perfected their combat moves so they could send any opponent flying. They worked together to build clever crime-fighting equipment and solve mysteries. They are friends and partners, and they have both pledged their lives to helping others.

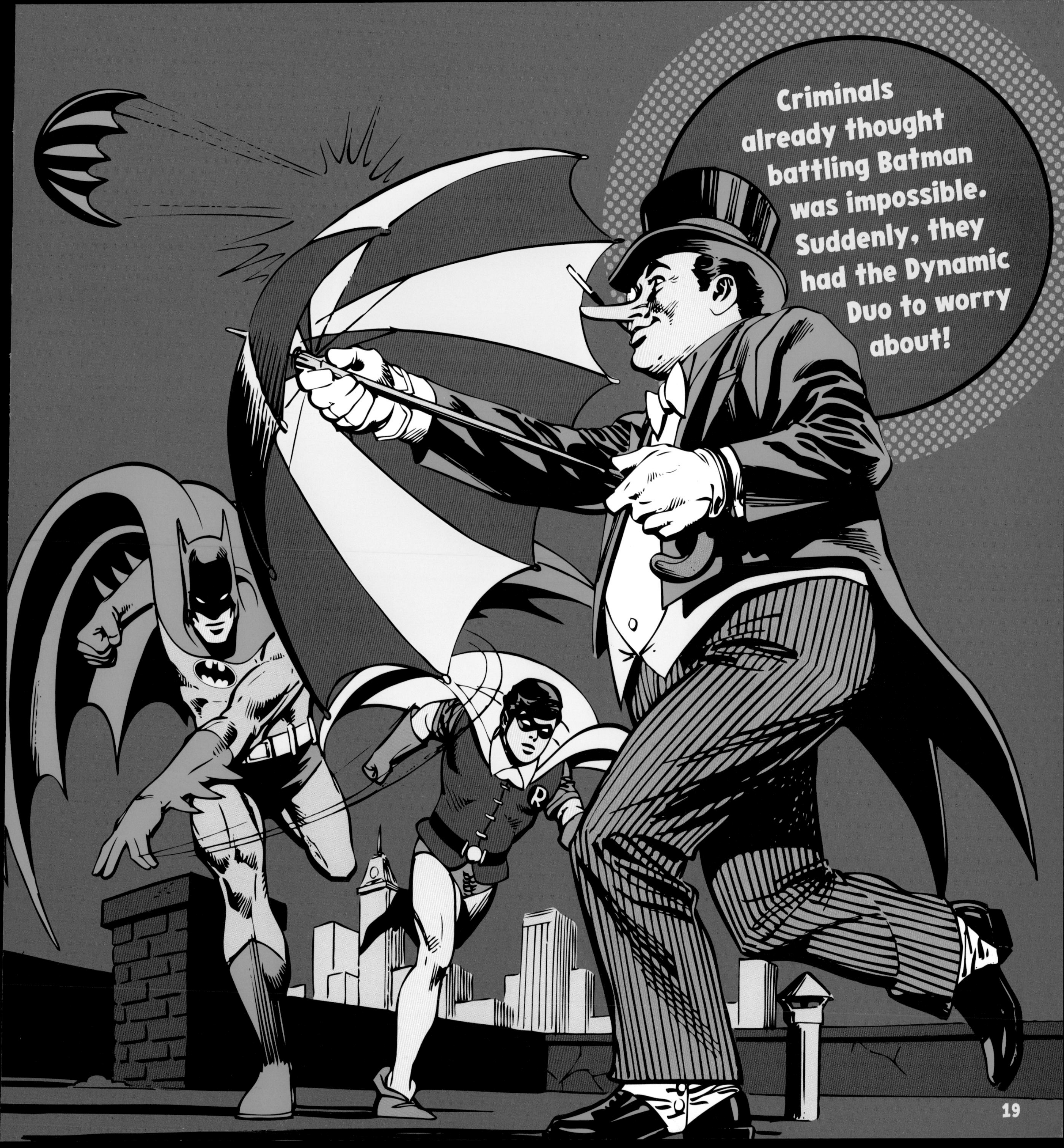

Criminals already thought battling Batman was impossible. Suddenly, they had the Dynamic Duo to worry about!

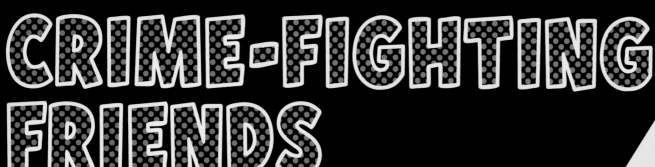

CRIME-FIGHTING FRIENDS

Batman and Robin couldn't do their job without help from some other close friends.

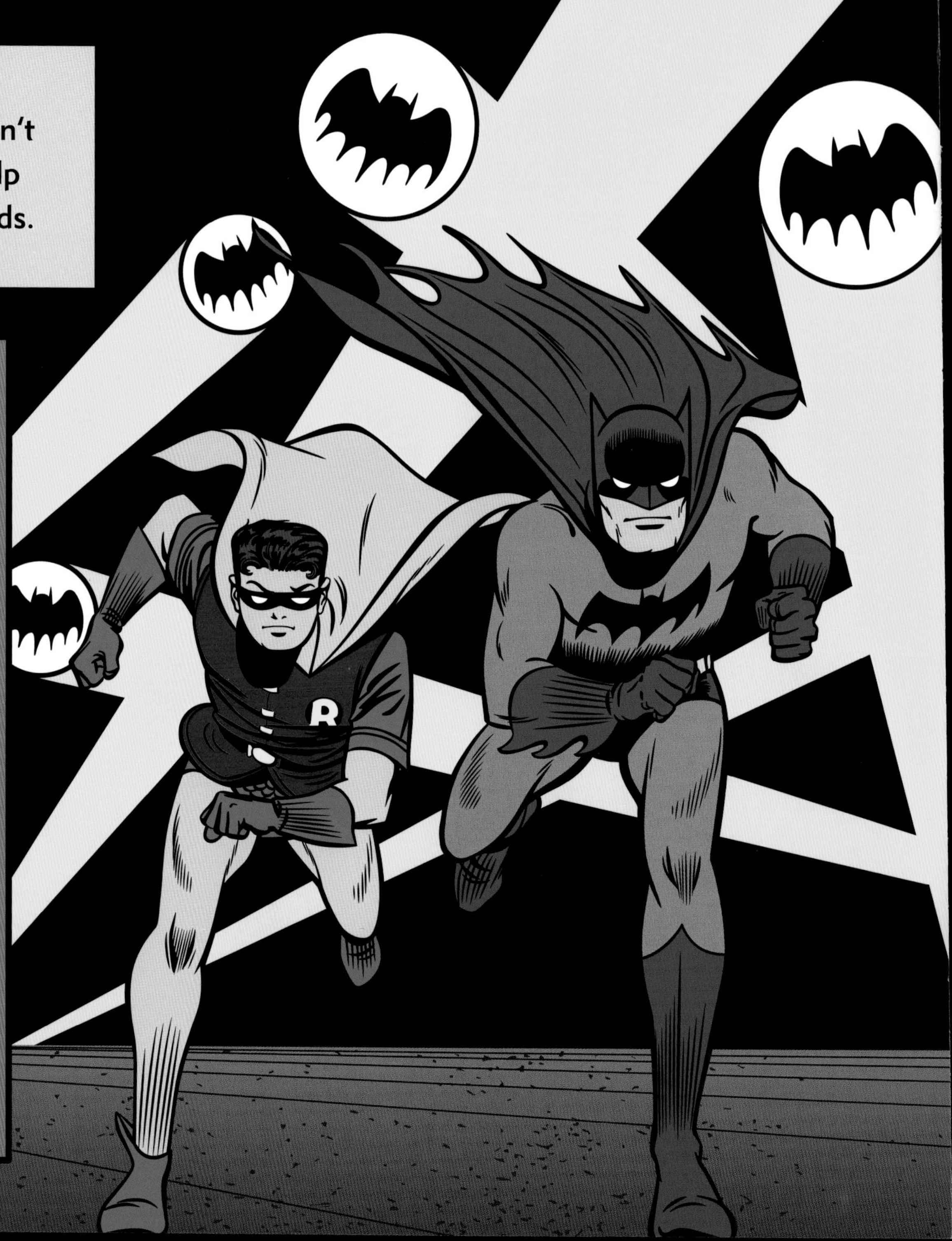

R

COMMISSIONER GORDON

Jim Gordon is the tough, dedicated head of the Gotham City Police Department. When he has a case that only Batman can solve, he shines the Bat-Signal into the sky and knows the Dark Knight will soon be on the job.

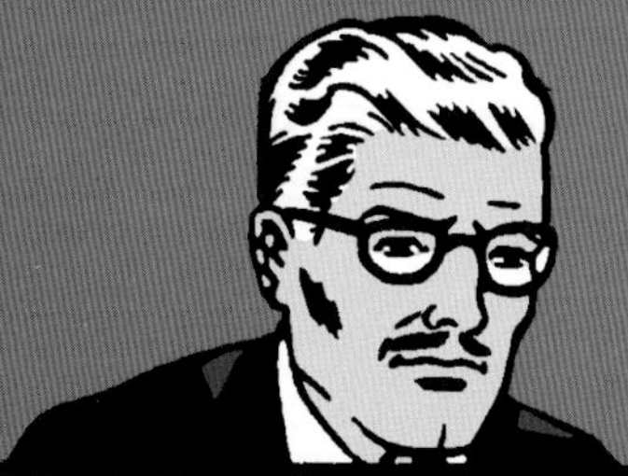

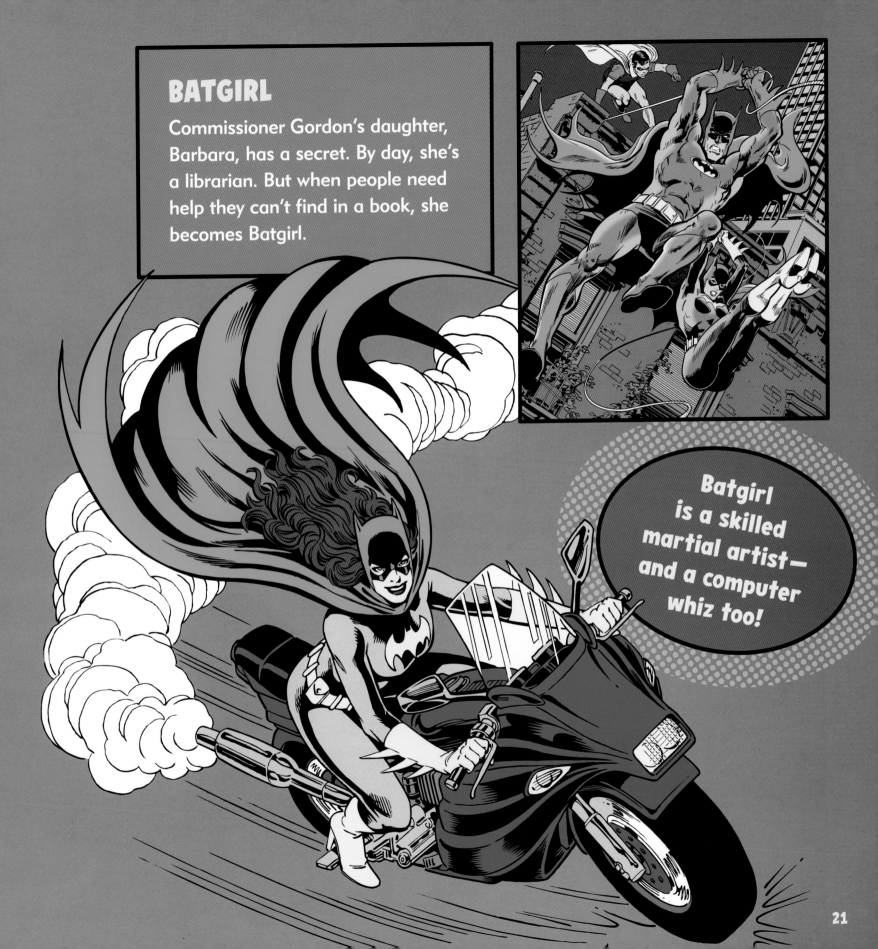

BATGIRL

Commissioner Gordon's daughter, Barbara, has a secret. By day, she's a librarian. But when people need help they can't find in a book, she becomes Batgirl.

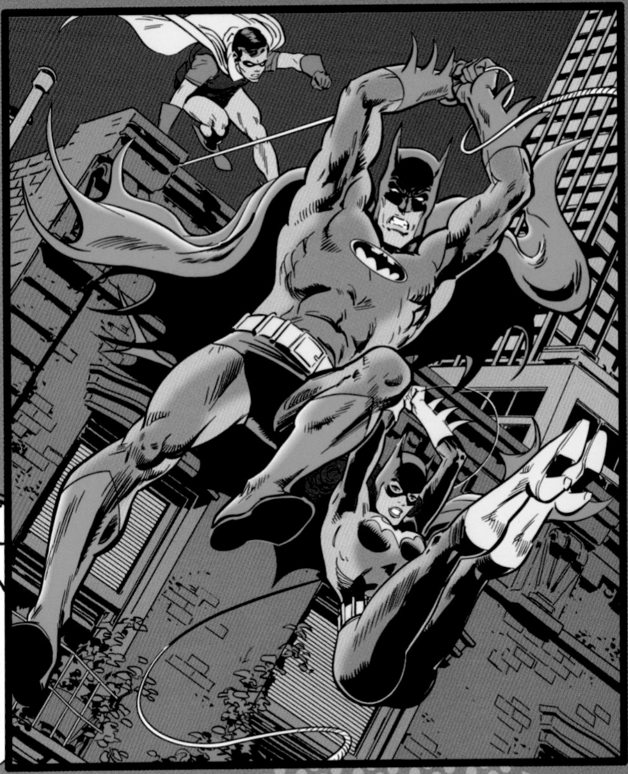

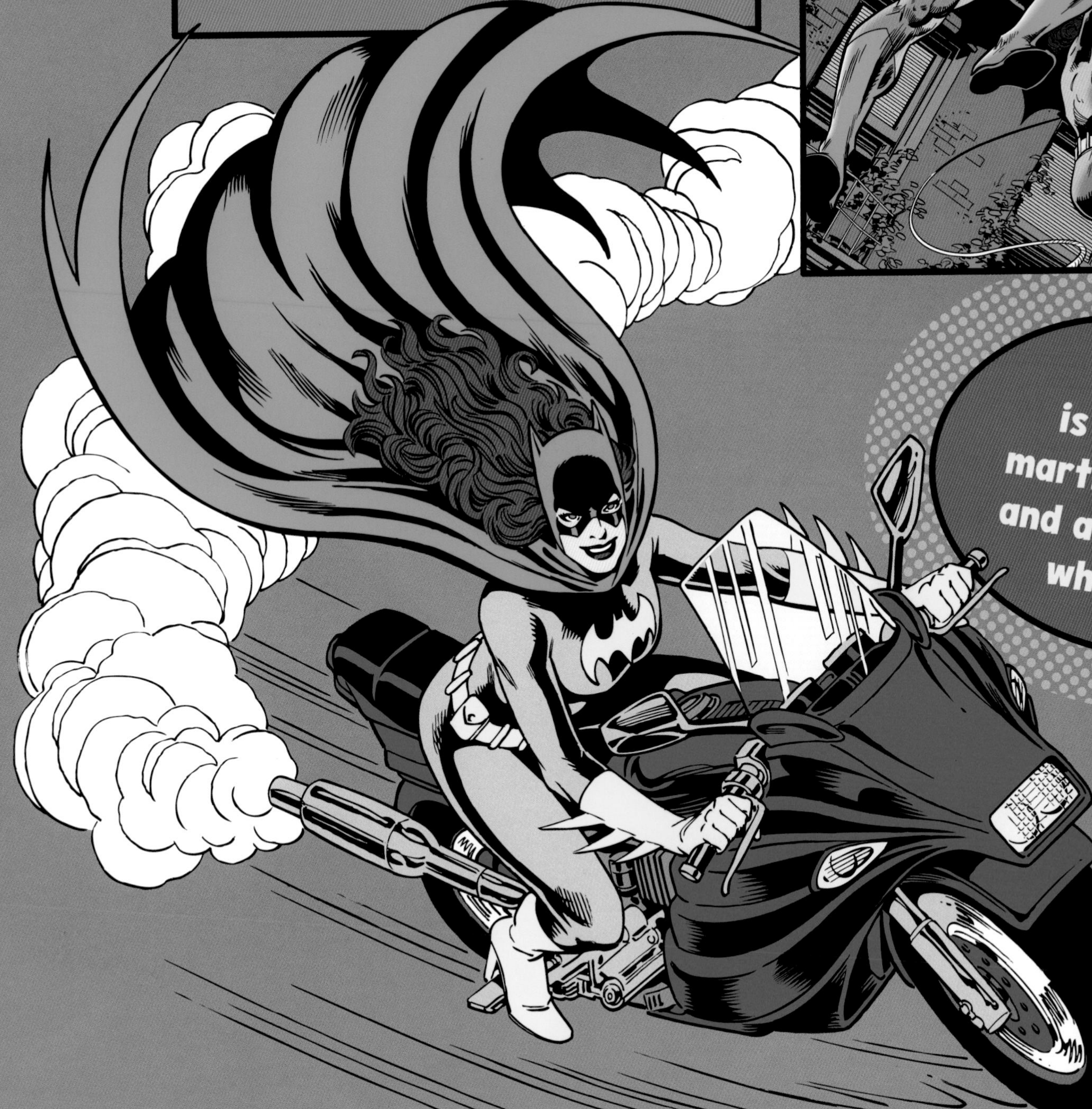

Batgirl is a skilled martial artist—and a computer whiz too!

When a crisis calls for more than one hero, Batman can team up with some awesome allies.

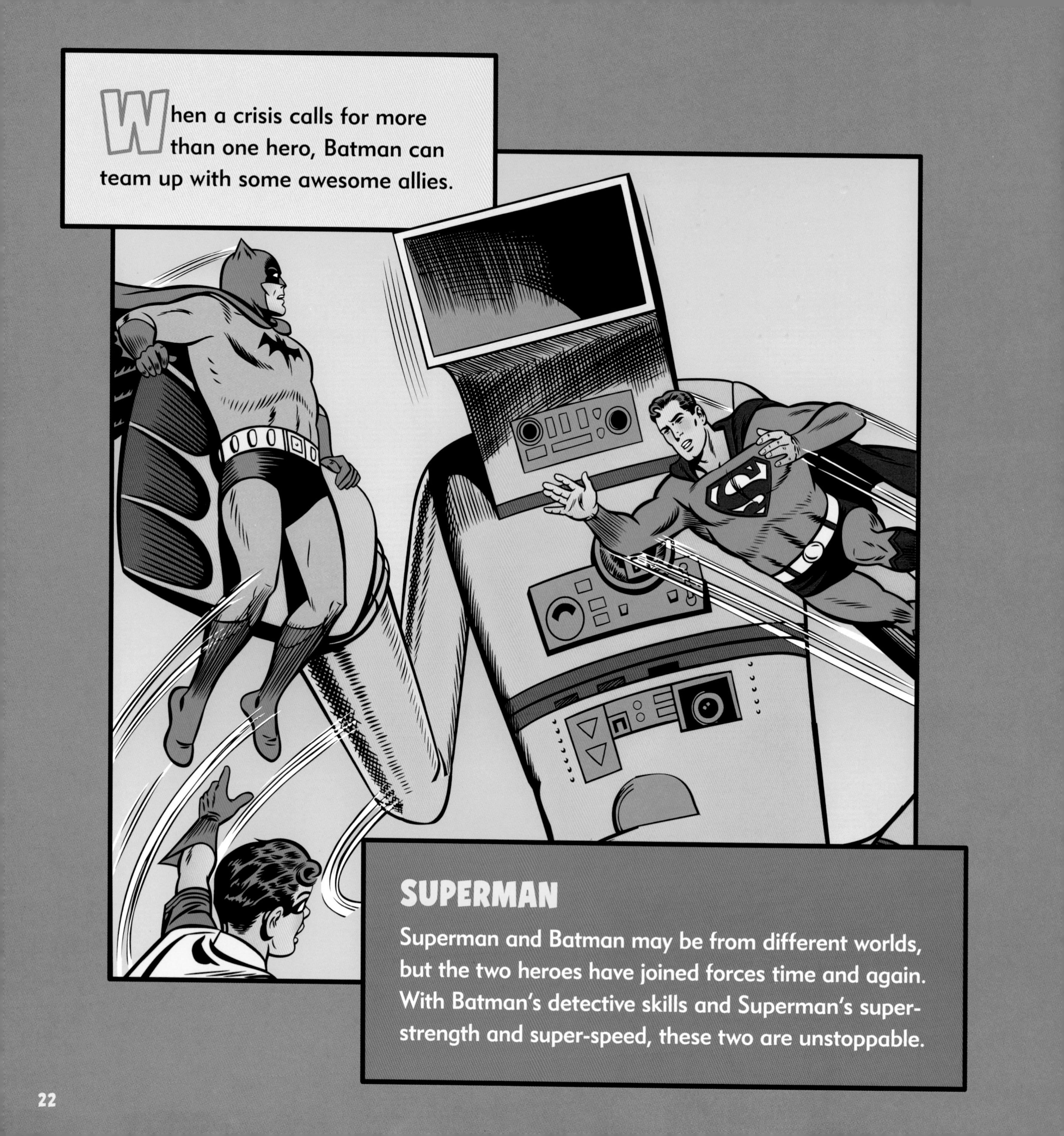

SUPERMAN

Superman and Batman may be from different worlds, but the two heroes have joined forces time and again. With Batman's detective skills and Superman's super-strength and super-speed, these two are unstoppable.

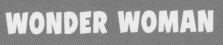

WONDER WOMAN

When Wonder Woman is around, Batman has a mighty ally in his fight for justice. She is a fierce Amazon warrior.

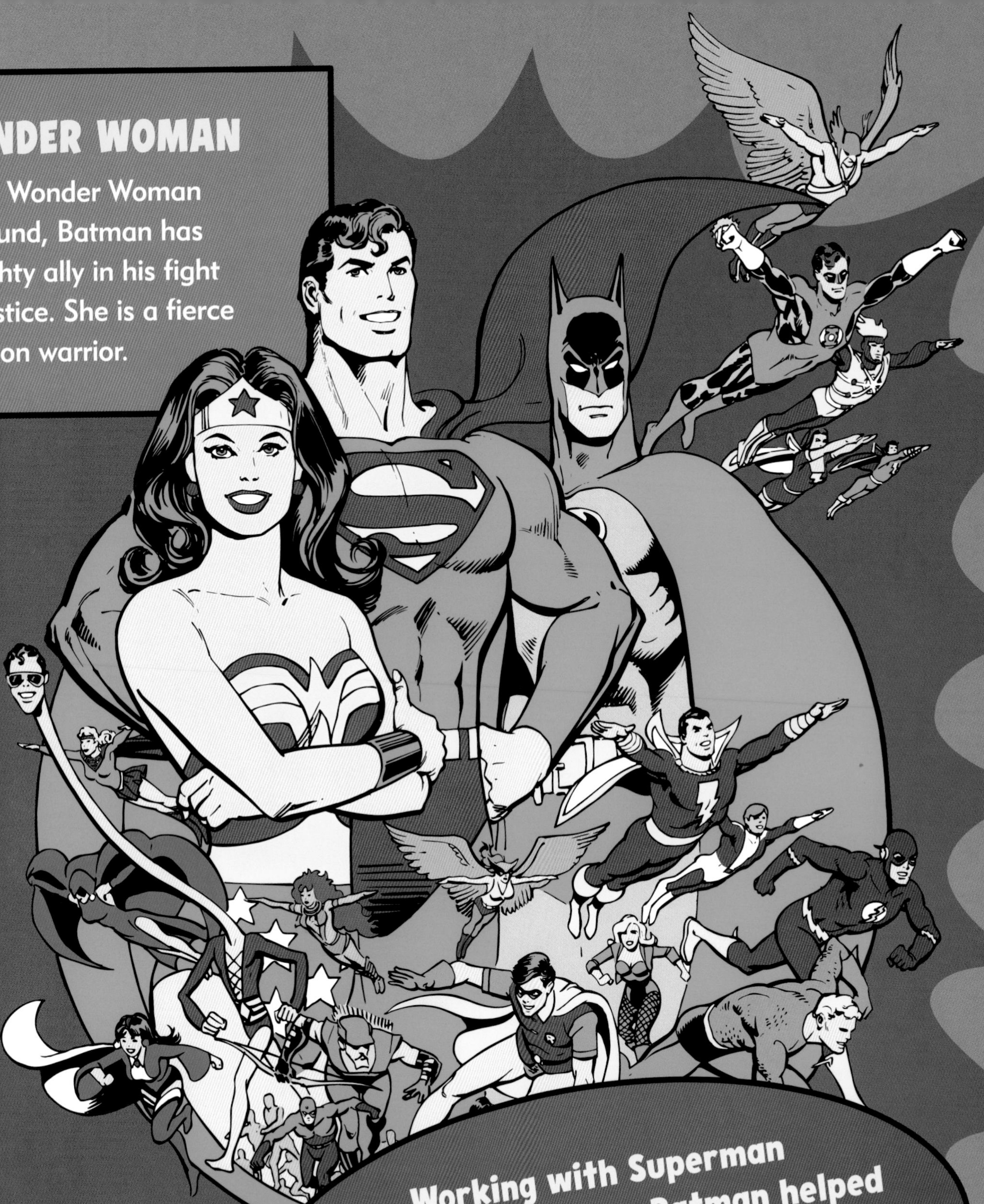

Working with Superman and Wonder Woman, Batman helped to start the Justice League, the greatest group of crime fighters in the universe.

THE FIENDS AND THE FOES

The villains Batman battles are a bizarre bunch.

THE RIDDLER

Before the Riddler puts one of his schemes into action, he leaves Batman a mysterious clue. If Batman can solve the riddle in time, he'll stop the Riddler's wicked games.

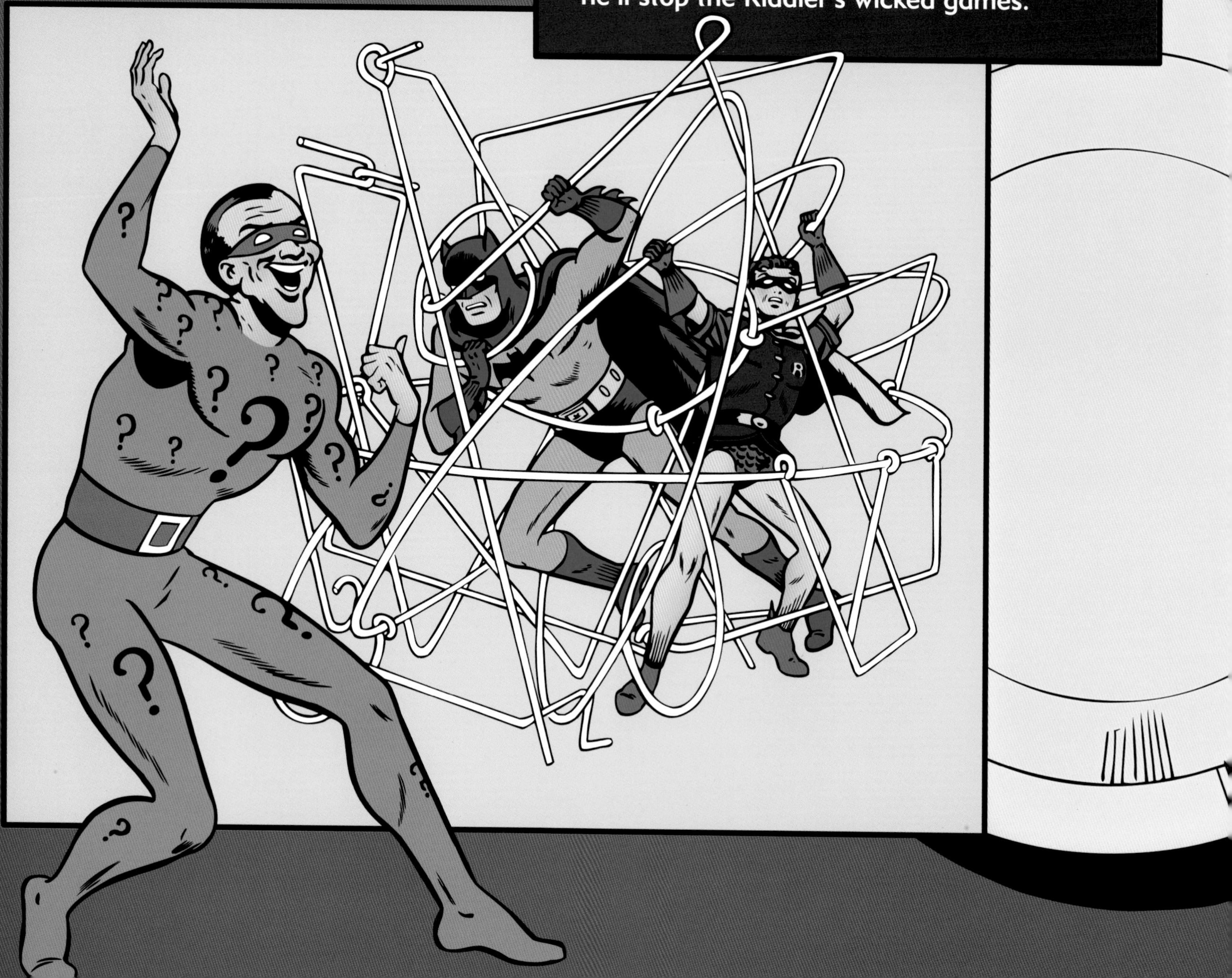

R

THE JOKER

This smiling fiend is no laughing matter! He terrifies the good people of Gotham as much as Batman scares the criminals.

They call the Joker the Clown Prince of Crime.

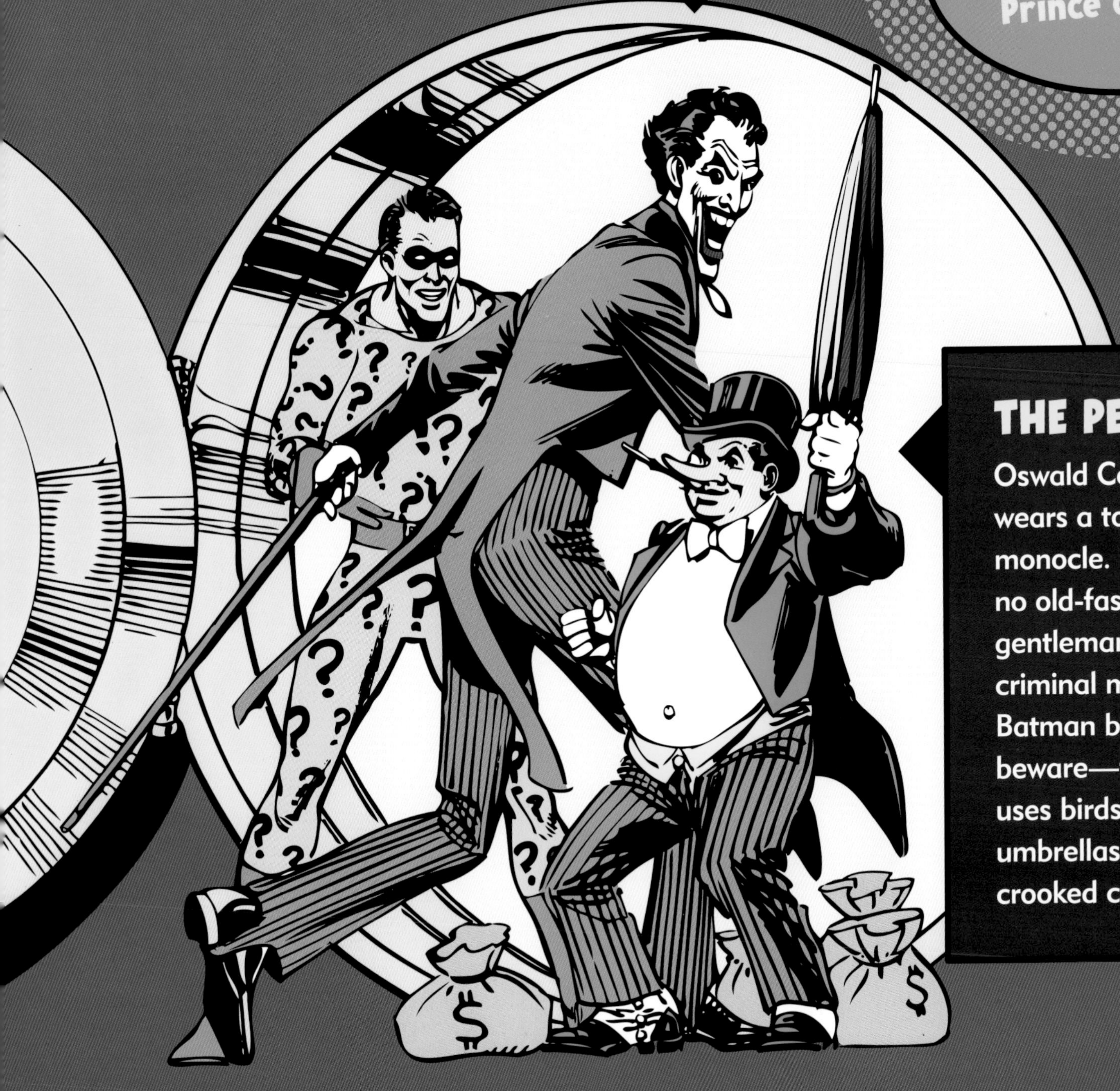

THE PENGUIN

Oswald Cobblepot wears a top hat and monocle. But he's no old-fashioned gentleman. He's a criminal mastermind! Batman better beware—the Penguin uses birds and trick umbrellas in his crooked capers.

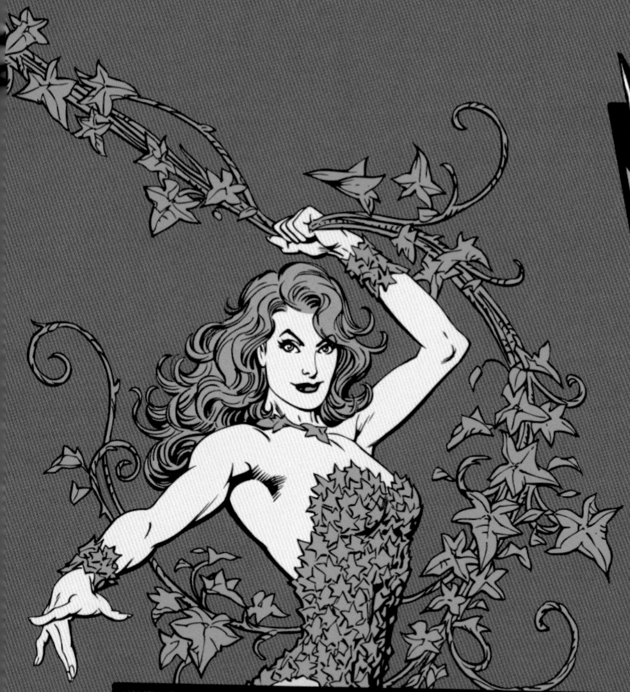

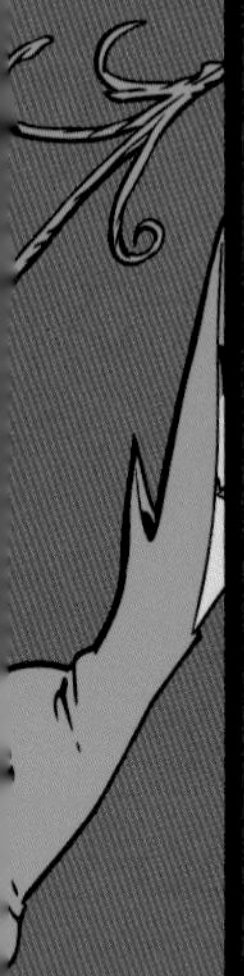

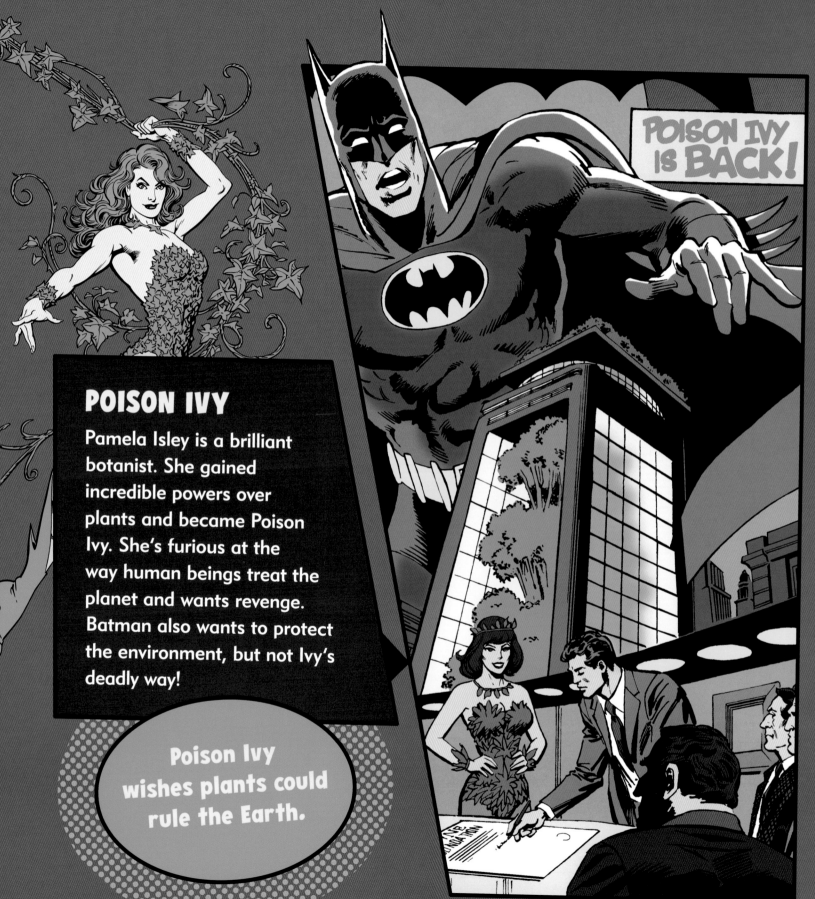

POISON IVY

Pamela Isley is a brilliant botanist. She gained incredible powers over plants and became Poison Ivy. She's furious at the way human beings treat the planet and wants revenge. Batman also wants to protect the environment, but not Ivy's deadly way!

Poison Ivy wishes plants could rule the Earth.

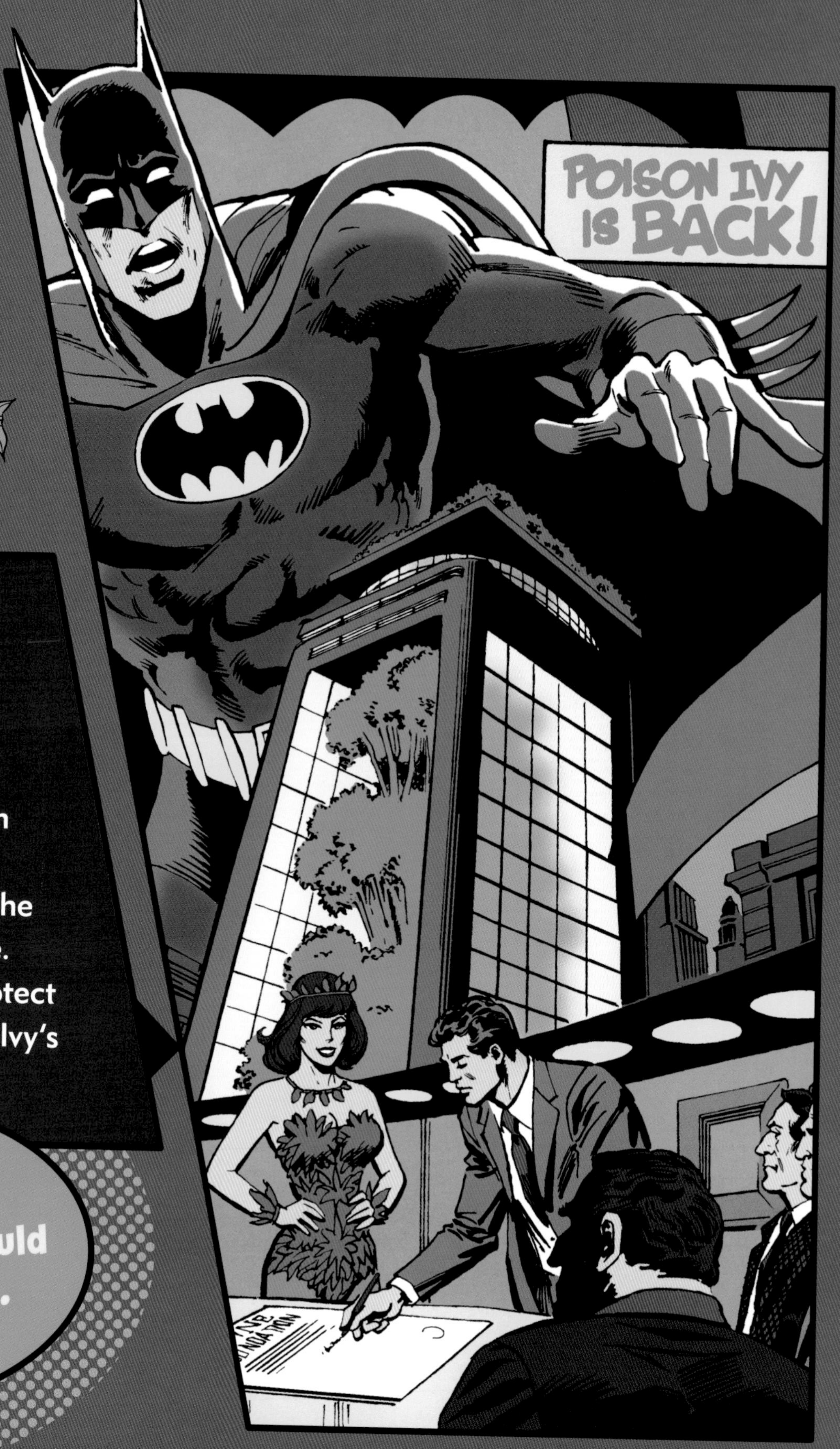
POISON IVY IS BACK!

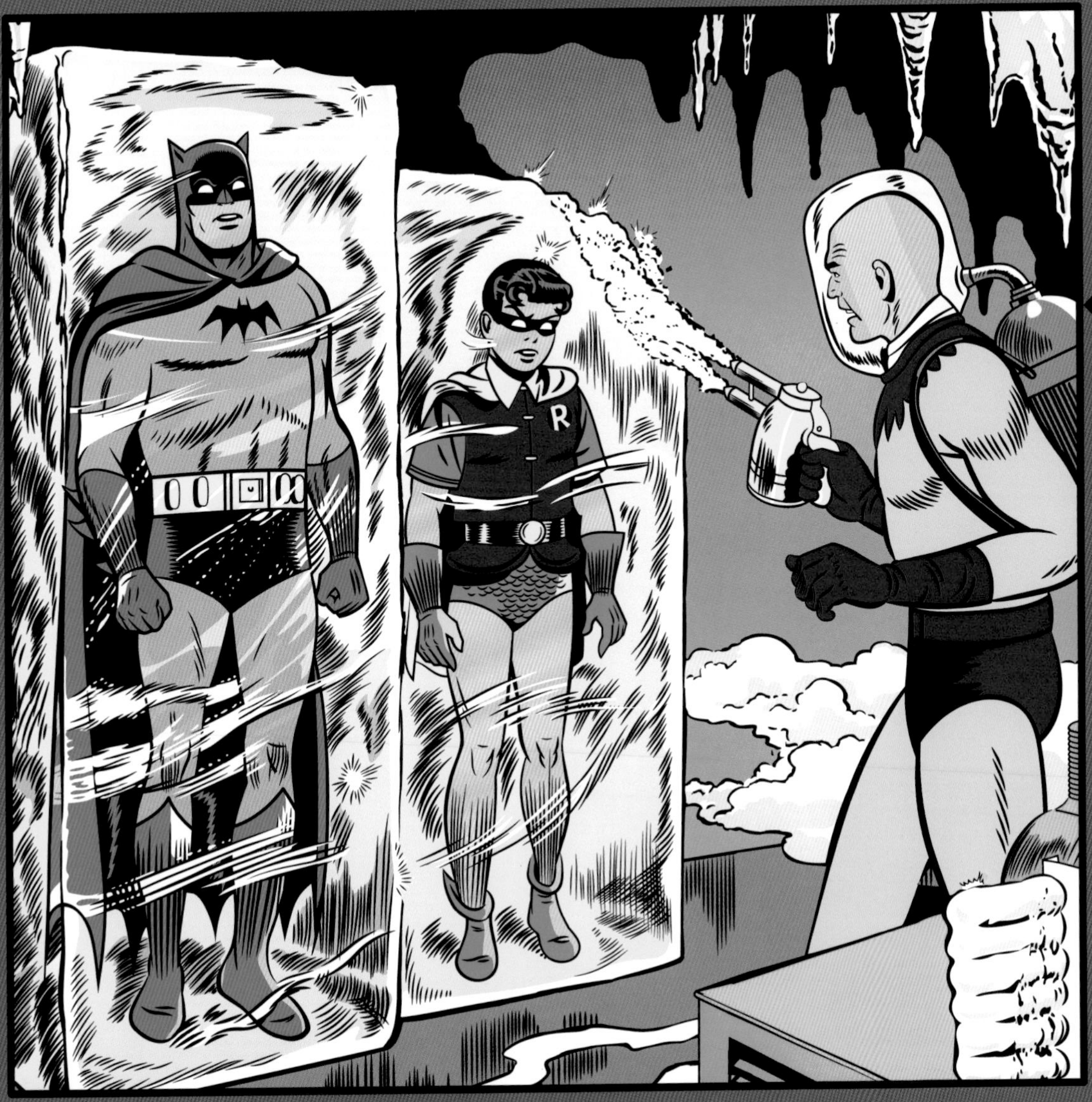

MR. FREEZE

This cold-hearted creep lives inside a refrigeration suit to stay alive. He uses frosty weapons to enact his chilling plans.

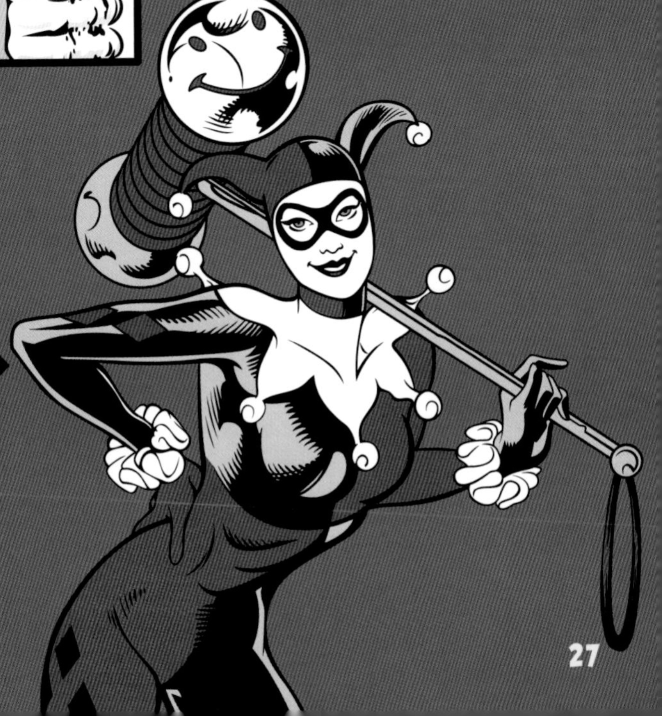

HARLEY QUINN

Heroes better duck when this madcap acrobat starts swinging her mallet! Harley is the Joker's partner and his equal in creating mayhem.

TWO-FACE

Harvey Dent was Gotham City's district attorney and Bruce Wayne's friend. But an accident left him half-scarred and all dangerous.

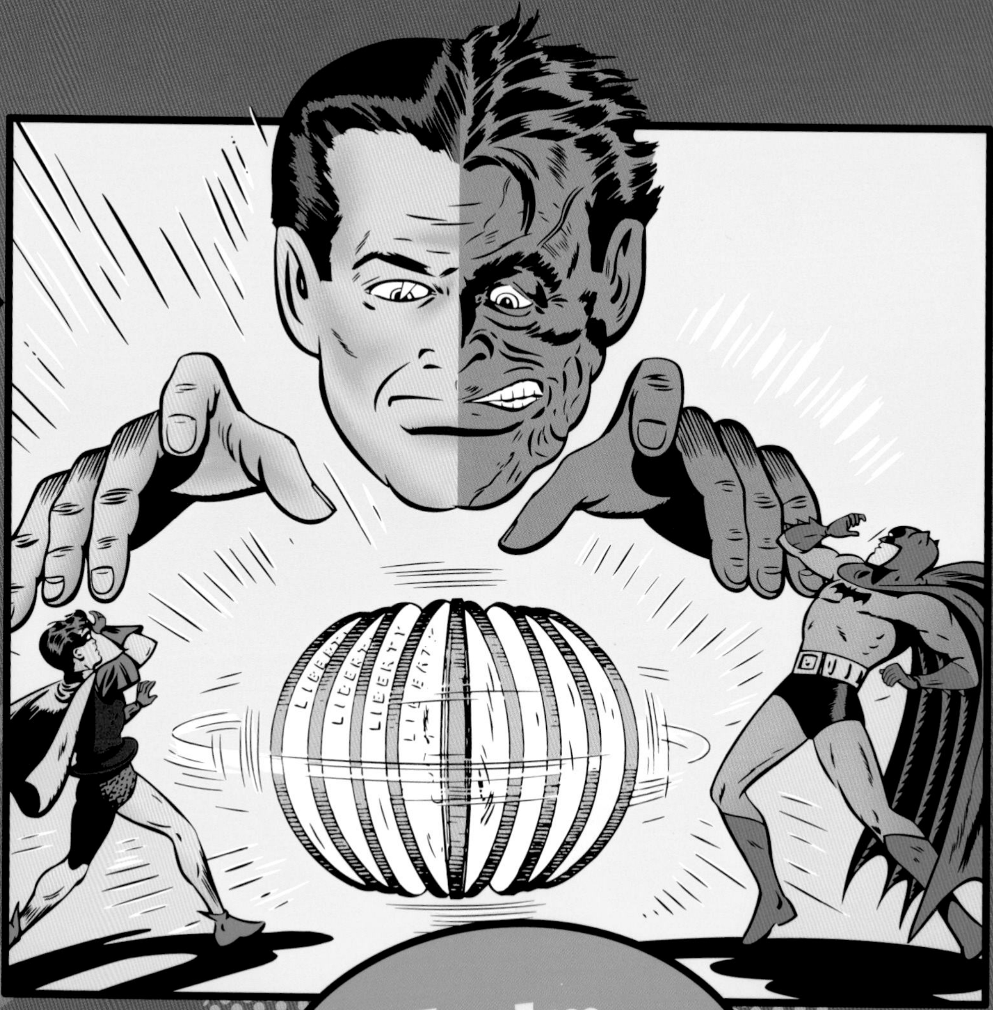

Two-Face flips a coin to choose between good and evil.

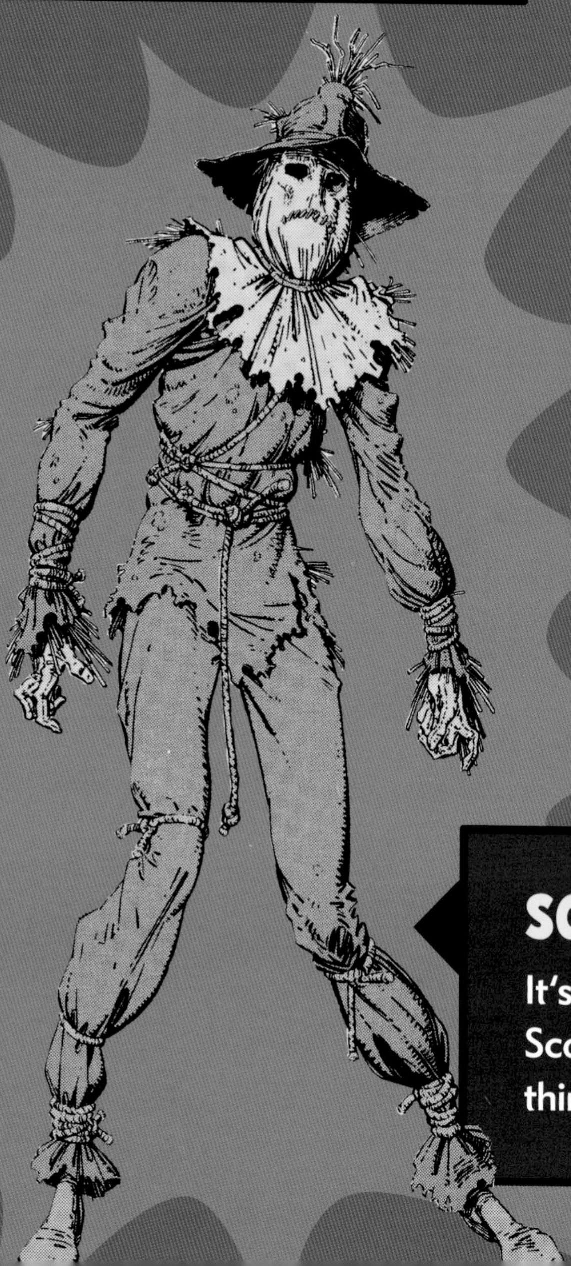

SCARECROW

It's not just birds who should fear this maniac. Scarecrow will spray fear gas that makes you think your worst nightmares have come true!

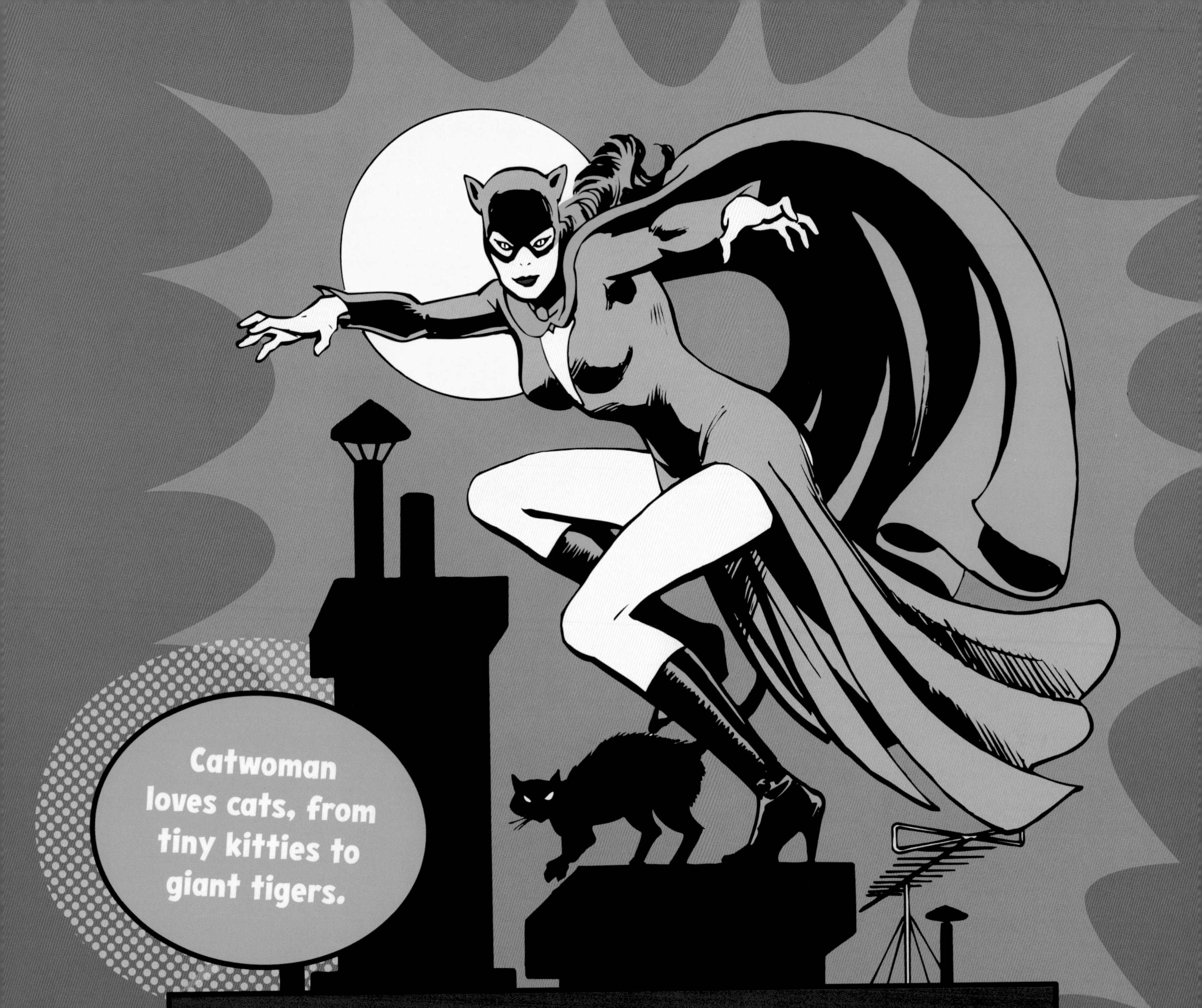
Catwoman loves cats, from tiny kitties to giant tigers.

CATWOMAN

Selina Kyle is the greatest cat burglar on Earth. But at times she has helped Batman. He hopes that, one day, she will leave crime behind and use her brains, strength, and catlike reflexes to be a force for good.

A CITY SAVED

Batman loves Gotham City. When he saw criminals taking over his hometown, he became a warrior for law, order, and justice. He smiles when he sees that the people of Gotham City feel safe to walk the streets.

Some people think Batman is crazy to do what he does. Others can't believe he is only one man. Batman doesn't mind. He doesn't need the people to understand him or even to thank him. He's just happy to help.

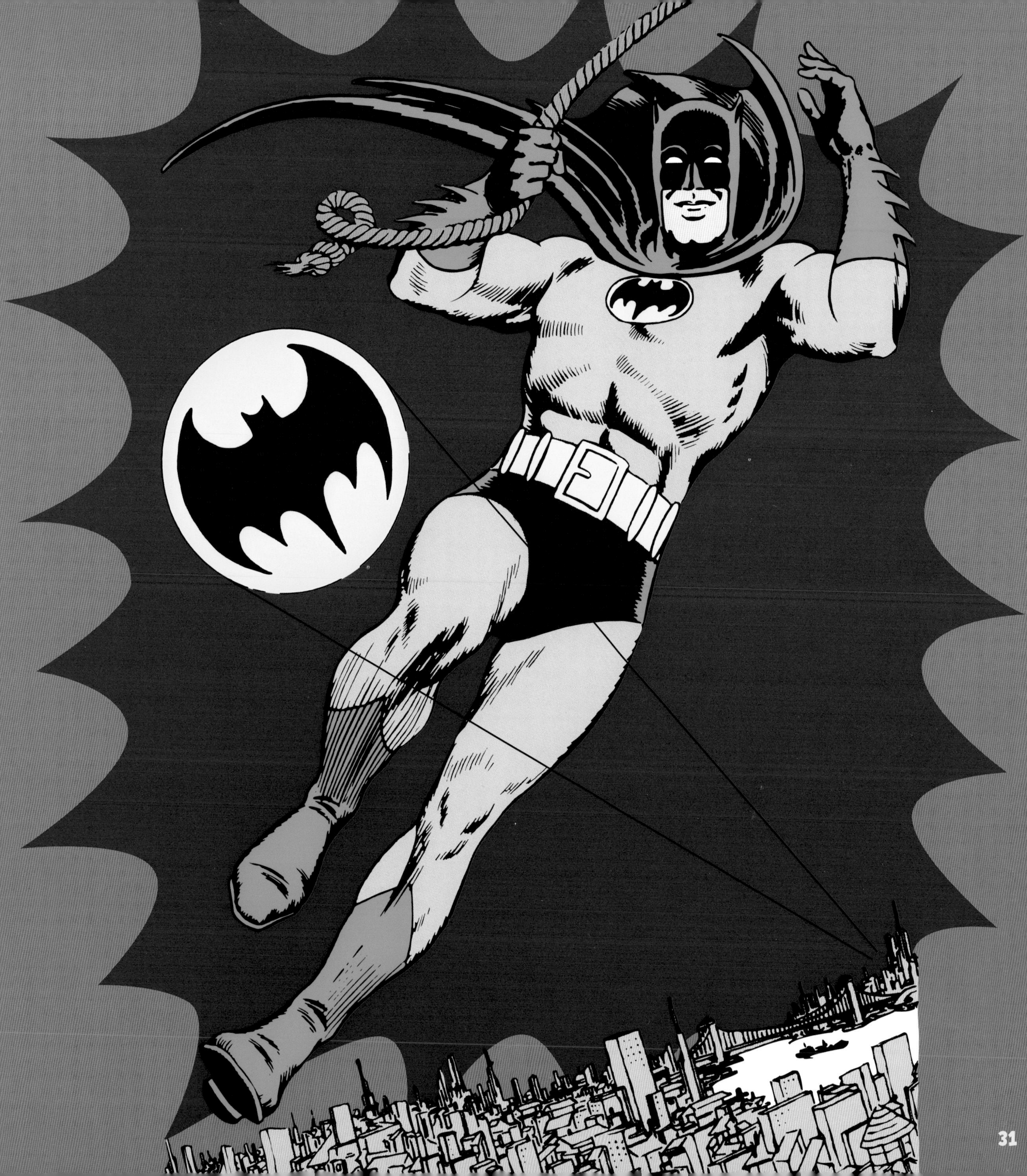

It took a lot of hard work for Bruce Wayne to become Batman. And he never stops striving to be the hero Gotham City needs. Along the way, he has met a lot of friends who help too. What are you striving to be? How can your friends and family help? What kind of hero are you?

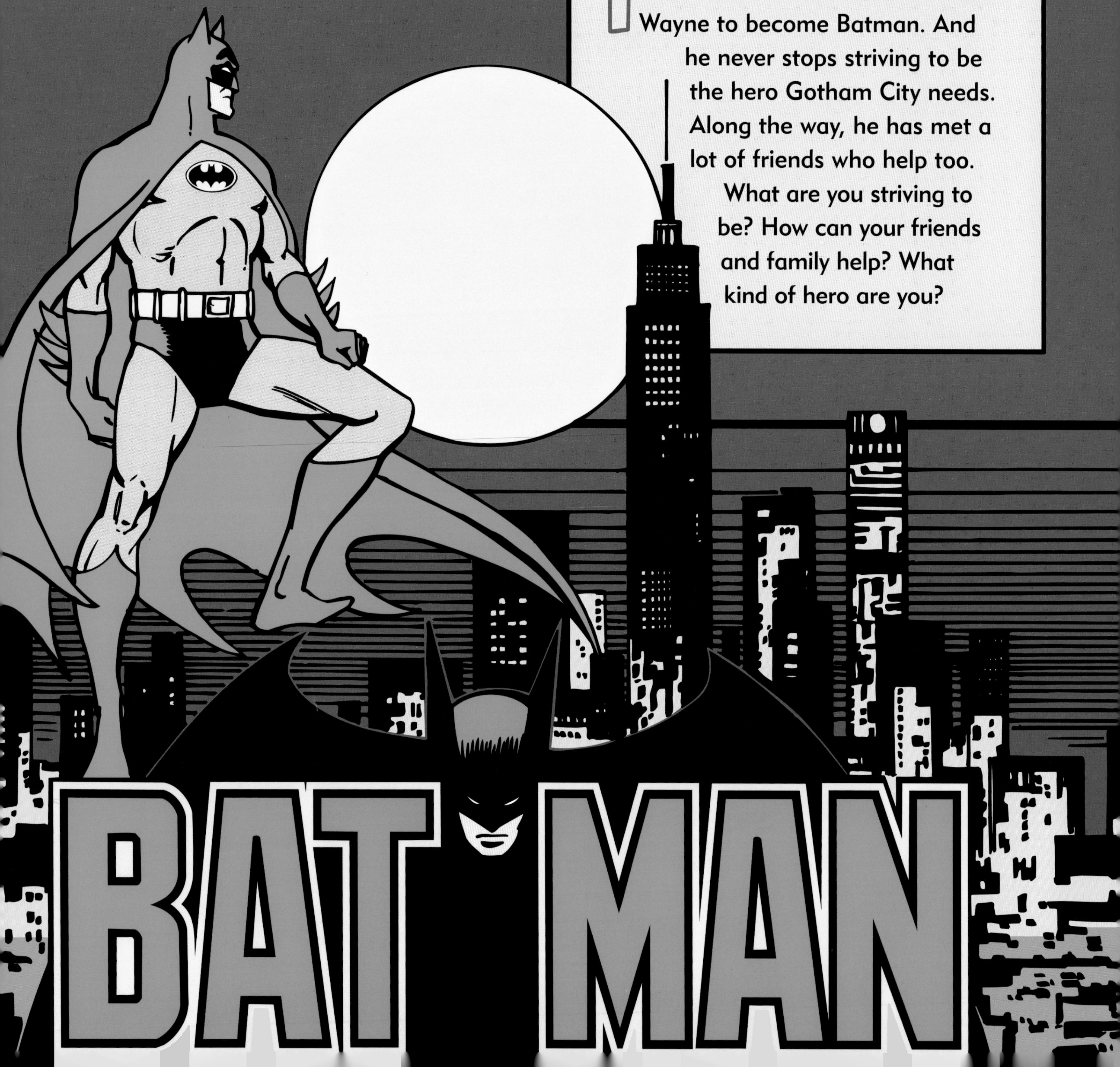
BATMAN